HOW TO SURVIVE
A SCANDAL

Christine Merrill

MILLS & BOON

First published in Great Britain 2022
by Mills & Boon, an imprint of HarperCollins*Publishers* Ltd,
1 London Bridge Street, London, SE1 9GF

www.harpercollins.co.uk

HarperCollins*Publishers*
1st Floor, Watermarque Building,
Ringsend Road, Dublin 4, Ireland

How to Survive a Scandal © 2022 Harlequin Enterprises ULC

Special thanks and acknowledgement are given to
Christine Merrill for her contribution to the
Society's Most Scandalous collection.

ISBN: 978-0-263-30194-6

10/22

MIX
Paper | Supporting
responsible forestry
FSC™ C007454

This book is produced from independently certified FSC™ paper
to ensure responsible forest management.
For more information visit: www.harpercollins.co.uk/green.

Printed and Bound in Spain using 100% Renewable Electricity
at CPI Black Print, Barcelona

To Mischief, the newest member of the family.

Prologue

26th June 1813

My dear Lords, Ladies and Gentlemen of the ton,
The London Season is nearing its end, but there is still time to share any salacious on dit or shocking revelation that would help us choose 1813 Society's Most Scandalous.

This Season, the Fitzroys and the Claremonts, who have so often entertained us with their long-standing rivalry, have been disappointingly free of dirty linen. The truce between the two families that began with last Season's scandalous marriage of Frederick Fitzroy to Lady Dorothea Claremont has been further cemented with the recent union of George Claremont to Miss Kitty Fitzroy.

If they will not entertain us, then who will rise—or sink—to take this year's prize?

Have your nominations delivered before the Season's closing party to The Times, *Fleet Street, London.*

The name of the winner of the ton's most eagerly awaited opprobrium will be published, as always, on the morning after the final ball of the Season.

Yours ever in scandal,

The Times *Society Editors*

Chapter One

On a road at the edge of the city, two carriages sat side by side, the spirited horses tethered to them dancing in anticipation. A few feet ahead, a lone man stood with a white handkerchief in his hand, set to signal the start of the race.

He gave a shout for silence, counted three and let the linen flutter to the ground.

Annie Fitzroy gave a snap of the reins and steadied herself against the sudden lurch as the horses began to pull. She snapped again, adding a twitch of the whip in her left hand, just enough to tickle the ears of the horses and urge them on.

It worked. They were galloping in no time, edging out the driver to the left. That fellow seemed to think that managing his beasts required brute strength and cursing. He was yanking on his own reins in a way that left the horses angry and confused.

She laughed and gave her team their head, pulling easily out in front at a breakneck speed that would have set a less experienced driver tumbling from the seat of the high-perch phaeton. As it was, the rush of wind around her took her bonnet, leaving her brown hair to blow in the breeze.

Claudine, her maid, would have a fit when she saw the condition of it, she was sure. But a little disorder to her coiffure would be worth it if she could manage to put Clive Whittacre in his place over his comments to her about the incompetence of women drivers. She glanced over her shoulder to see him exactly where she'd hoped he would be, squarely behind her with no hope of catching up as she passed the mile marker that stood for a finish line.

Then, she slowed to a stop, pulling off to the side of the road to give her competition more than enough room for his own ungainly finish, tugging up her gloves and patting her hair into place as he jumped down to help her from her seat.

'Damn—I mean, dash it, Lady Anne, but that was a fine bit of driving.'

'Then, sir, I take it that you retract your earlier statement that all women are a menace on the road and should be banned from touching the reins.'

Her opponent laughed. 'I amend my statement, at least. You should be banned from racing so as to give the rest of us fellows a sporting chance at winning.'

She gave him a nod of approval and one of her best society smiles, the sort that would probably have him trailing after her at the next ball, eager to make this event into something far more than it was, a simple contest of skills.

It was a shame she was not interested in him. It was not as if she meant to reject any man who could not best her in a race. But she did not see herself marrying someone who mistreated his horses and Mr Whittacre had a heavy hand with the whip.

Her brother, Freddie, separated himself from the little crowd of onlookers waiting at the side of the road and came towards her to take possession of his carriage. 'You have got to stop doing this,' he said, handing her her bonnet, his smile tinged with exasperation.

'Doing what?' she said, doing her best to appear oblivious to the men around her and their expressions of shocked interest.

'Besting my friends at their favourite pursuits,' he said with a shake of his head. 'It is most unladylike of you.'

'I will stop when the gentlemen stop giving me reason to compete,' she said with a shrug, offering his whip back to him. Then, she settled her hat on her messy hair and tied a smart bow under her chin. 'It is not my fault if they insist on acting superior to impress me. I cannot resist proving them wrong.'

'The least you can do is lose once in a while,' he said, digging in his pockets for sugar lumps to award the winning horses. 'Perhaps it was my mistake for bringing you to Tattersall's today. Exposing you to such an environment gives you ideas.'

'Ideas,' she said with a shudder, blinking her wide blue eyes at him and doing her best to appear feminine and therefore harmless. 'God forbid a woman have those. And as for Tattersall's, where else am I to get a decent mare? You have no idea what sort of nag I would be stuck with if Father made the choice for me. I am twenty, but he still treats me like an infant.'

'He would look for something safe,' her brother said reasonably.

'And where would be the fun in that?' she replied. 'I can handle anything on four legs as good or better than you can.'

'Have you forgotten that the goal of a London Season is to get you someone on two legs, not four? If you seem too wild, we will not be able to convince men that you will make a biddable wife.'

'My manners are fine enough, when I need them to be,' she assured him. 'And I am more than popular in the ballroom. Perhaps you were too busy courting Dorothea to notice, but I have had several offers already from men who admire my spirit.'

'Then why didn't you take them and save us all from worrying? Now that Hattie and Kitty are out of the house, I am sure that Mother and Father are at their wits' end that you will be left disappointed and alone at the end of the Season.'

'I will be far more disappointed if I choose wrong and settle for a man who doesn't love me as Hattie and Kitty's husbands do them,' she said with what she hoped was a non-committal shrug. There was no point in letting Freddie see that she found the subject somewhat worrisome as well.

It might have been easier to come to a decision if everyone around her was not so spectacularly happy with the partners they had found. At this point, she had been flattered, fêted and danced about the floor by every eligible man in London and none of them had made her heart flutter, much less pound in the way Hattie and Kitty had described to her. Was it too much to ask for a match like the ones she had seen her family make, with genuine love and affection on both sides?

'Mother and Father do not want me to rush into a bad marriage, I am sure,' she said, not sure at all. She had been receiving gentle hints from both of them that it was time to choose a favourite. But how could she do that when no one stood out from the crowd?

'You do not have to do it today,' Freddie said, probably noting the worried look on her face. 'But the least you can do now is to accept the congratulations of your many admirers. If there is a man here not angling after you since this latest stunt, I will eat my hat.'

'Very well,' she said with an impish smile. 'I suppose I can force myself to be admired, since I was actually quite wonderful.'

She walked over to the group of friends that had witnessed the race and was more worried than flattered when the first man to come forward was the last one whose attention she wanted to attract.

Montgomery James was a rake. Though some might argue that he could be reformed by the love of a good woman, Annie was not that naive. If she could not find an honourable young man to marry, she had no intention of throwing herself away on a dishonourable one.

But that did not stop her from flirting when the opportunity presented itself, which it often did.

'Lady Anne,' he said with a wolfish smile. 'That was an impressive display of horsemanship.'

'Don't you mean horsewomanship?' she said with a demure tip of her brim.

'On the contrary. No man could best you,

therefore the word suits even such an attractive person as yourself.'

'Then I will accept the compliment,' she said, 'though it is hardly adequate to compare me to such a fallible creature as the male of the species.'

At this, he laughed. 'We are horrible, are we not? But what would you do without us?'

She was tempted to tell him that she was likely to discover that if someone did not step forward with a suitable offer. Instead, she laughed back to assure him that her criticism was all in fun.

'But surely you deserve some sort of trophy to celebrate your win. And your opponent has given you nothing.'

'Alas, no,' she said, regretting that she had not bothered to wager.

He reached into his pocket and held out his closed hand to her, waiting for her to offer her open one. When she did, he dropped an unmarked gaming token into it. The thing was black as jet and just as heavy, intriguing in its simplicity. She held it up to admire it and waited for an explanation.

'I am having a little party at my club this evening. All the smartest people will be there.

You are invited, of course,' he said with a magnanimous gesture. 'Just show the chip at the door to gain admittance.'

She laughed and shook her head. 'I have heard of the sort of parties you throw, Mr James. They are hardly appropriate for young ladies of good character.'

He sighed. 'How dreary it must be to be one of those. But in this case, you need have no fear. The event I am planning is of a different nature than you may have heard. It is a salon, rather like the ones held in Paris.'

'That sounds intriguing,' she admitted.

'You will enjoy it, I am sure. The conversation will be lively and the company good.'

'I will consider it,' she said with an ambivalent nod. 'And now, if you will excuse me?'

'Of course,' he said, lifting her fingers to his lips for a brief kiss.

She responded with a polite smile and withdrew her hand. While it might be amusing to flirt with Mr James, she knew better than to take his advances seriously. He was far too big a scoundrel to believe that there was anything permanent in his attentions to her. Nor did she think his party was likely to be as he described it.

Still, the idea of a salon interested her. Perhaps she could organise a gathering of artists and poets herself. She would need to find someone like Lord Byron, but not so tiresome. Someone society had not already grown weary of...

As she was considering possibilities, Lady Felicity Claremont approached her. As usual, she was grinning like a cat in cream, probably having thought of some way she could draw the attention of the group back to herself. Annie was unsure what she had done to make the girl so competitive, other than to be a Fitzroy and thus the object of all Claremont envy. It seemed that that family could never be satisfied with their own august place in society, always hankering after and talking about what Annie's own family said or did.

But since the rivalry between the two houses had gone on for two generations, there was nothing to be done for it but to endure. Today, she forced a smile and said, 'Felicity', in the most welcoming tone she could manage.

'Anne,' she said in return, with the faintest edge to her voice, 'you have made quite the spectacle today with your driving.' It was plain that Felicity was the lone member of today's crowd that was not impressed by the race.

'Thank you,' she said with a smile, then straightened her bonnet to show that she found nothing particularly negative about making such a splash.

'Of course, you always do need to be the centre of attention,' she added, to make the censure clear.

'When they are out for their Season, no young lady wants to go unnoticed,' Anne reminded her.

'That is not a thing that I need to worry about,' Felicity said with satisfaction. Then she held up a black gaming token, letting it shine like a little circle of night in the bright sunlight. 'You are not the only one to catch the eye of Montgomery James.'

Annie looked at the thing incredulously. She had not really expected that she was the only one he'd invited, but it surprised her that he would prey upon one so naive as Felicity Claremont, who was eighteen and in her first Season. 'I do not know that it is a thing to be proud of. It is certainly not an invitation to be acted upon, without great risk to one's reputation.'

'And yet you accepted it without question,' the other girl said with an arch of her eyebrow.

'Only to be polite,' Annie replied with a cool smile. 'Reckless though he may be, Mr James is a friend of my brother's and his club is frequented by most of the high fliers in London. The men, at least,' she amended. 'I cannot think of a single girl in my acquaintance who has ever been there.'

'All the more reason that we should act on our invitations,' Felicity said, holding out the chip as if she could lure Annie forward like a dog to a bone. 'Of course, if you are too afraid...'

'I am not afraid,' she said quickly. It was less a matter of fear than it was of common sense. She had bribed her maid to give her an explanation of what happened at such parties and, although it had been most enlightening, it was not something that an unmarried female should know about, much less experiment with. At least, not for the sake of Montgomery James. The man was as slippery as he was handsome and several young ladies had already come close to ruining themselves trying to secure his attention.

In the end, she shook her head at Felicity and smiled.

'It does not matter either way. I am previously engaged this evening and would not think of crying off the musicale we are to be attending for a night of dubious fun.'

At this, Felicity laughed. 'I am invited to the same party. It will be a dead bore and you know it. These things always are. But maybe you would shine better there than in a party of sophisticates.'

'I do not need attention,' Annie said, surprised at the rebuke.

'Really?' Felicity replied, glancing at the carriage which Freddie was driving back to the start of the race.

'I did not think…' Did people really think of her as craving applause? She had not meant anything by it, other than to get Whittacre back for his comment and to run for the joy of speed. But apparently Felicity saw it another way.

She took a deep breath, trying to shake off the faint feeling of hurt. 'All the same, I would not risk going to Mr James's party. It is not what he describes it as and I am sure I would not like it.'

'Perhaps you will not,' Felicity said with a toss of her head. 'I shall send your regrets when I see him tonight.' Then she turned and walked away.

Captain William Grosvenor was both sick and tired.

Sick in soul and body and tired of life. Or perhaps it was life that had tired of him. After taking a ball to the shoulder in a French attack, he had been treated like an invalid and bundled off to London to recuperate. But though his arm got better each day, the cure continued to be more painful than the disease. There were problems here that he could not solve with an armed battalion and he was not sure he was up to them.

'If you go back to Spain, what are you going to do about the house?' This question came from his friend, Andrew Fairfax, who was following him down Jermyn Street like a particularly annoying puppy.

'What you mean to say, Andrew, is "Condolences on the death of your brother",' he responded in a dry tone.

'Edward has been dead for some months,' Andrew reminded him. 'It is not that we do not regret his passing. It is that we have got rather used to him being gone.'

'Whereas for me, it is a recent loss,' Will responded, annoyed. It had been difficult getting any news from home when he had been on the front and, since letters from Ed had been rare, he had not noticed when they had stopped entirely. 'I had no idea...' He trailed off.

Not until he had been forced home by his wounds. And now, everyone expected him to take on an estate he did not want without allowing him a moment to grieve. 'I hate it here,' he muttered, unable to help himself. Ed had always loved London, its crowded buildings, its throngs of people and the endless bustle of the Season. And London had loved him in return.

But Will had joined the army fresh out of Oxford and never looked back. In Spain, there had been no one to compare him with Ed and to find him wanting. He had found his place and been happy there. And then, it had ended.

'You are the head of your family now, but you have not mentioned any plans to settle down and marry. That is why I—we,' Andrew corrected, 'wanted to know about the house.'

Andrew stood to inherit a manor and did not really need a house. But at the moment, he was living under his father's roof and was eager for independence. It was probably why he was willing to run over Ed's grave to snatch the keys out of Will's hand. It was unseemly.

'While I am here, I intend to live in it,' he responded. It was more than he needed, but it made no sense to let rooms and leave it stand empty.

'But you are going back to Spain,' Andrew reminded him.

'I do not have my orders yet,' he said trying to ignore the ache in his right shoulder. 'I will go to the Horse Guards tomorrow and we will see.'

'I—'

'I am not ready to discuss it,' Will said, cutting the conversation short.

'Well, are you willing to talk about what we are doing tonight?' Andrew said in a frustrated tone. 'It is not healthy for you to be shut up alone every evening.'

'I prefer solitude,' he insisted. It gave him time to think. Too much time, probably.

'You would like the city better if you bothered to sample some of its entertainments,' Andrew insisted. 'It is far more civilised than a battlefield and just as exciting.'

'You do not know,' he responded, thinking of Spain and the men there, still fighting. It was not excitement he craved. It was a sense of purpose. In London he felt useless and adrift. 'I do not belong here.'

'You do not belong because you do not try,' Andrew said.

'I have tried,' he insisted, 'and found it insufficient.' More accurately, he was the one that could not live up to society and this time it was more than his arm that failed. All he knew was that the cold, distant, blank spaces in his body and heart refused to be tempted back to life by the sort of common pursuits that interested Andrew.

But whatever it was that weighed him down must not be visible from the outside. Andrew certainly did not notice the change in him and now he gave him an affectionate cuff on the arm, forgetting the pain it might cause. 'You think too much about the war. What you need is a diversion. Something to take your mind off your own troubles.'

He supposed that Andrew meant liquor or women, or both. 'I have had more than enough of what you are suggesting and it has made no difference.'

'Not like this,' his friend said with a laugh that had the very devil in it and hinted at all the temptations Old Scratch might promise. Then, he reached into his pocket and produced a black gaming token. 'This is what you need. A ticket to Montgomery James's gaming hell. The stakes are high, the liquor is smooth and the women are pretty and plentiful. His parties are known all over London for tempting even the most jaded tastes.'

Will sighed. 'I am not jaded.' But if not that, then what was he to call what he was feeling? It was embarrassing to admit that the prospect of whores stirred nothing in mind or body but a kind of sick dread and a fear that his body would fail in the act as it had the last time he'd tried it.

Still, he took the token, weighing the smooth black chip in his hand. 'Is this place truly so different?'

'I guarantee it will change your life,' Andrew replied.

'I will expect nothing less,' Will said and tried to believe that it could be true. He needed something, some way to get his strength back, so he might be the man he once was. But what that elusive thing might be, he did not know. Perhaps tonight he would find just the something, or the someone, he was missing.

Chapter Two

~~~~~~~~~~~~~~~~

The soprano warbled in front of her and Annie tried not to squirm in her seat. As Felicity had predicted, the evening was already boring and the music had barely begun. Worse yet, when she turned around to catch a glimpse of the Claremont family, Felicity was conspicuously absent.

As one solo followed another, the absence of the other girl preyed on her nerves. She would not have gone to Mr James's salon, would she? Surely she would not have been so stupid as to take that invitation. If so, it might be the ruin of her.

When the intermission finally arrived, Annie approached Lady Claremont to ask after her daughter and was told that Felicity had stayed home with a megrim.

'I sympathise,' Annie said, trying to quell the unease that the news raised in her. 'I feel something similar.' Then, after a great show of touching her temple and wrinkling her brow, she went to find her mother and ask that the carriage be summoned to take her home.

'Are you sure you do not want me to accompany you?' her mother asked with a worried expression.

'No need,' she said, trying to look more wan than nervous. 'I mean to go straight to bed. There is no reason to spoil your evening over that.' And that was exactly what she hoped she would be doing, after she had assured herself that Felicity was where she was supposed to be.

Once in the carriage, she directed the driver to take her to the Claremont home, where she was met by a baffled butler who assured her that Lady Felicity was still out for the evening, at a musicale with her parents, and was not expected back until late. Annie thanked him and hurried back to her own home to plan her next move.

What was she to do about this situation? It

did not really concern her but, all the same, she felt responsible for it. If Felicity hadn't been so intent on besting her in something, she might have thought twice about accepting Mr James's invitation. But now that she had, she likely regretted it and was in need of rescue.

But suppose she was not? Suppose that the party was exactly as Mr James had said, an innocent intellectual evening. She would look quite foolish if she sent Lord Claremont there to retrieve his daughter from a place where there was no risk. And if the party was as she thought, such a rescue might lead to scandal and ruination for Felicity.

She withdrew her own black chip from its place in her bedside table and was examining it when her maid came into the room to put her to bed.

When Claudine saw it, she released a torrent of French and shook her head violently. 'That is from Mr James's club. *Il est horrible.*'

'I know,' Annie said sadly. 'And I fear that a friend of mine is in great danger because of him.' Perhaps it was an exaggeration to call Felicity a friend, but tonight Annie felt responsible for what she had done and strangely close to her.

'Then we must do something to help her,' the maid said, wringing her hands. 'The club is no place for a gently born girl.'

'How would you know such a thing?'

'I have a friend who sometimes works there,' she said with a dark look that hinted at what that work might include.

'And if I wanted to go to that party and retrieve my friend without scandal, what would be the best way to do it?'

'Mon Dieu,' Claudine said, then paused to think. 'We must dress you as a maid. You might enter through the back door and find your friend. Then, find my friend, Justine, and ask her for the best way to get away again. She will be in one of the bedrooms above stairs and, for your sake, I hope she is alone.'

'Thank you,' she said, giving her maid's hand an affectionate squeeze.

She allowed herself to be dressed in the simple gown of a servant and tucked the black token in her pocket, in case it was needed. Afterwards, she called for the carriage and was soon delivered to the back door of Montgomery James's club.

She told the servants at the kitchen door that she was a maid for one of the guests and needed to find the lady's retiring room, for that seemed like the most logical place to begin her search.

The cook rolled her eyes at the words, but announced that she was to go through the main rooms and up the stairs to the first bedroom on the right. Then, she was shooed out of the kitchen and through a green baize door to the party.

The sight of it shocked her so much that she nearly ran back to the safety of the kitchen. Mr James had promised her a refined party where none but the best would attend, but this was nothing of the kind.

Except for the candles on the crowded gaming tables, the room was dark, the air thick with tobacco smoke and the smell of spilled liquor. Everywhere she looked, she saw men weaving on their feet from excessive drink, shouting and laughing over dice and slumped insensate on the furniture. None of the women in the room was of her acquaintance. Their faces were painted and their dresses were indecently low. These supposed ladies hung on the shoulders and about the waists of the male guests, urging them on in whatever vices they had chosen. From their husky laughter she suspected cards and dice were not the only games they were willing to play if the gentlemen were so inclined.

If she wanted to survive with her reputation intact, she had to get out of here without being recognised. If Felicity was here, she must find her as well. She might claim to be worldly, but the younger girl would have no idea what to do when faced with such obvious depravity.

Annie ducked her head and kept to the shadows, working her way around the edges of the room and towards the stairs. But she was mortified to find that some of the corners were occupied with amorous couples who had not bothered to climb the stairs to find a bed.

She shielded her eyes against the sight of too much exposed flesh, flashes of white breasts and even whiter bottoms, and the sound of bawdy giggles, and hurried on, racing for the stairs.

When she arrived at the retiring room, she darted inside, slamming the door and staring at the women inside who stared back at her in curiosity. With their revealing gowns, painted faces and teased hair, Annie stood out among them like a pigeon in a flock of peacocks.

Then one of the ladies let out a sigh of frustration and said, 'Good God, there's another one. What are we expected to do with them?' Then they parted to reveal Felicity on a *chaise* in the middle of the room, her eyes round with shock and her shoulders trembling.

'I have come to take Felicity home,' Annie said, grabbing the other girl's hand.

'I did not realise...' Felicity said with a helpless shrug.

Annie did her best to hide her frustration for she had warned the girl of exactly this possibility. But recriminations would do no good, so she patted the other girl's hand and murmured, 'It is all right. We will not speak of it now.' Then she looked to the other women in the room. 'Claudine said I should ask Justine for help in getting away.'

A pretty blonde woman stepped from the back of the circle of courtesans and gave a nod of acknowledgement. 'Do you have a carriage?'

'I sent it away,' she said with a shake of her

head. 'I did not want the equipage with the family crest to be seen lingering here.'

Justine gave her a pitying look. 'Some of the best families in London are prone to *linger* here. Just not with their daughters. But if you do not have a ride home, we will have to find you one.'

Suddenly, the door opened and a man half entered, then stopped to lean on the doorway as if he had just realised he was in the wrong room. By his bright red coat and the braid on his sleeve, Annie could tell he was an army captain and a strikingly handsome one at that. His brown hair was neatly cropped, his blue eyes twinkled, and his chest was as broad and solid as a brick wall. She wanted to lean against it and sob with relief.

He glanced from face to face with a sheepish grin. 'Begging your pardon, ladies. I mistook the door.' Then his eyes lit on hers.

And that was what it felt like. A sudden beam of sun shining in a dark world. She wanted to walk into that light, to bathe in them like sunshine after rain. Then his smile turned to one of invitation, and she remembered where she was and said, 'No!'

He drew back in surprise as if the last

thing he'd expected to find in this room was rejection.

He was about to go when she remembered that, above all else, she and Felicity needed help. And she could not bring herself to believe that this man was like the ones she had seen downstairs. 'Wait!'

At this, he grinned and offered an unsteady bow. 'For you, dear, anything.'

'Are you an officer and a gentleman?'

He laughed. 'I did not think to be called such in this place, but I suppose I am, when the situation calls for it.'

'There is a lady in need of assistance,' she said. She was likely a fool to rely on a stranger, but there was something about this man that inspired trust.

He bowed again, his movements more precise as he tried to shake off the effects of whatever he had been drinking. 'Then I cannot refuse. How may I be of assistance?'

'My lady and I need to get away from here, as quickly and discreetly as possible. Do you have a carriage, sir?'

'Not of my own,' he admitted. 'But I could summon one, if needed.'

'Could you do so and provide us safe passage out of this place?' she asked.

'At your service, Miss…' He left the sentence open, waiting for her to introduce herself.

'Annie, sir,' she said and dropped a curtsy like a proper maid.

'Annie,' he said. 'And I suppose your mistress will remain nameless.' He scanned the room behind her, searching for the woman she spoke of.

'If you please, sir,' she said, falling into the role of servant and stepping aside to reveal Felicity.

He let out a low whistle. 'I was promised an unexpected diversion, but I did not know it would be a member of my own family, trapped behind enemy lines and in need of rescue.'

'Cousin William,' Felicity moaned and collapsed back on the *chaise* in a shower of tears.

'I've a good mind to tell your father where I found you,' he said in a stern voice.

'Please, do not. I promise this will never happen again,' she said, eyes wide and expression earnest.

'Very well,' he said with a sigh. 'At least

you had the sense to bring a maid.' He looked from one to the other of them and said, 'I may have drunk enough rum to sink a pirate ship, but I think I can manage to sneak you down the back stairs.' Then he offered his arm to Felicity and said, 'We will soon have you out of here and on your way home.'

She hesitated, casting a desperate look at Annie as if fearing the punishment that would befall her if anyone learned of this visit.

Annie gave her a firm smile and said through clenched teeth, 'Yes, my lady. We must be going now. Take your cousin's arm and let him lead us out.'

She required no further persuasion, but seized the Captain's elbow in a death grip and let him take her from the room with Annie following one step behind. But rather than taking the main stairs, he was leading them past the bedrooms and further into the house.

'There must be a servants' stairs around here somewhere,' he muttered and tried the door at the end of the hall. 'Here we are. Dark as pitch, but leading down. Mind your step, Cousin.' They came out in the kitchen and he shepherded the pair of them through the back door and on to the street, walking them to the corner where carriages for hire waited.

'Let me give the gentleman your direction,' he said to Felicity. Then, to Annie's surprise, he climbed into the coach after them.

'You needn't accompany us further,' Annie assured him, not wanting him to see where she was going.

'Surely you do not begrudge me a seat in the carriage I am paying for? Perhaps I would like to visit the Claremonts and have a little talk with the Duke.'

At this, Felicity burst into tears again, and hid her face in her hands.

He pulled a handkerchief from his pocket and handed it to her. 'Do not fear, Cousin. I will not be telling your parents where I found you. I will not even ask why you were there. In fact, I think the less said on the matter the better. But I trust I will not have to save you from there again.'

Her tears stopped just as quickly as they'd begun. 'No, William,' she said in a quiet voice. Then she went back to looking out the window.

Annie leaned back into the corner of the carriage, both relieved and mortified by the way things had turned out. Since this William was a member of the Claremont family, they were in no danger at all. But neither had it been necessary for Annie to rush to the rescue of a girl she didn't even particularly like. It was possible that the Captain might have found her and got her home without Annie getting involved at all.

They had ridden in silence towards the Claremont house and when they arrived, Felicity hopped out of the carriage and rushed up the steps to her house, leaving Annie alone with the Captain.

'Well, Annie,' he said giving her a wolfish smile, 'aren't you getting out? This is your home as well, is it not?'

If she wanted to keep her disguise in place, she really should get out here as well and make some effort to pretend that she was Felicity's maid. But the night was long and her feet were tired and she just wanted to go home without having to explain anything. So, she sat there in silence, waiting for the Captain to speak again.

'I thought not,' he said, folding his arms and giving her a critical look. 'You may dress like a maid, but if you are one, then I am Arthur Wellesley.' Then he tapped his stick against the box to tell the driver to continue driving.

She folded her arms and looked back at him with the same sullen look he was giving her. It hardly seemed fair that a man who had knowingly attended that bacchanal had any right to chastise her for wandering into it by mistake.

'Not talking?' he said with a knowing nod. 'Then allow me to have my say. I do not like being lied to, especially not by silly girls. You were very foolish to be there at all and you are lucky that mine are the only hands you fell into.'

'I am aware of that,' she said, 'and thank you for your help.' He deserved gratitude for what he had done because he had arrived at the moment they'd needed the most help. But if he was expecting an apology, he could go hang. She owed him nothing since she had only been there to help his even more foolish cousin.

His look, which had been expectant, turned annoyed. 'You express no contrition at all, do you? What guarantee do I have that you will not run right back into trouble when I let go of you?'

'It is not your job to worry about me,' she said.

'But it appears that someone should,' he replied. 'You are running riot about London in the middle of the night with strange men.'

'Are you strange?' she said with a smile. 'Because you seemed normal enough when I asked for your help. Worse for drink, of course,' she added with a frown, since she was not the only one behaving badly.

'You have no right to question my behaviour, which was a damned sight better than the other men at that party.'

'That was likely only because it was early,' she replied. 'The men at that party were all there with the same thing in mind, I am sure.'

'And what would you know about that?' he said, surprised.

'Because I was hired to be there,' she said, seizing on the only lie she could think of that would explain her presence at the party. 'I am a friend of Justine's. That is why I was in the room where you found me.'

'You are a courtesan?' he said with a laugh.

'Yes,' she said, annoyed at his doubt. Surely

he was not implying that she wasn't pretty enough to serve as one.

'Dressed like that?' he said, staring at her maid's dress.

'I had just arrived,' she insisted. 'I hadn't changed into my work clothing yet.'

'Your work clothing?' He scanned her up and down as if trying to imagine her in a scandalous red gown.

'It is not as if I can walk down the street with my bosoms exposed and my cheeks painted,' she replied. 'People would talk.'

'Next you will be telling me that whores wear uniforms,' he said, shaking his head.

'They do… I mean, we do, in a sense.' She waved a hand about her face to indicate paint and feathers, then gestured down her body to her breasts before quickly putting her hands in her lap. 'How else would you know us?'

'By your behaviour, I should think,' he said.

'Really, sir,' she said with a disapproving shake of her head, 'do you not know that the way we act is all pretend? We want something from you and you from us. We act accordingly when we need to. But when we are not working?' She gave him what she hoped was an insouciant shrug. 'Then, things are quite different.'

'I see,' he said with a suspicious narrowing of his eyes. 'You are telling me that I found you in a room full of whores and just down the hall from God knows what in the bedrooms, because you belonged there.' His expression turned dark in a way that was probably supposed to be frightening. 'At any moment, a drunkard might have seized on you and given you the same as he gave the other ladies there.'

'But then you arrived,' she said, trying not to think of what might have happened. 'And I helped you to get your cousin away from there.'

'And thank you for that,' he said in a gentler tone. 'But in exchange for my help, I lose an evening of fun and am out the fare for the coach.'

'I will pay you,' she said, reaching for her reticule and remembering that she had not brought it.

'Will you now?' he said, his smile turned wicked. 'And when has a lightskirt ever said those words? It is completely against your nature to pay in money. But you can give me something that will make up for the trouble you caused.'

'What do you want?' she said, embarrassed at how small and helpless her voice sounded.

'A kiss should be sufficient,' he said. 'If you have embarked on a career as an adventuress, surely you will not begrudge an old soldier that.'

'You are not old,' she said, leaning back in her seat. He was young and vigorous, though he seemed to favour his left side as he reached for her. And the unexpected thought came to her that kissing him might be quite nice.

But there was the fact that this was a cousin of the Claremonts she was flirting with. Members of that family always seemed to be underfoot, causing trouble whenever they could. The last thing she needed was this newcomer spreading word around the *ton* that she was the sort to attend wild parties and kiss strangers.

'Afraid?' he said, grinning at her. 'I thought a woman of your experience would not be bothered by such a small request.'

'You are mocking me,' she said, lifting her chin in defiance.

'Not at all,' he replied. Then he blocked

the carriage door with his foot so there was no escape and beckoned to her. 'You are not going anywhere without paying the toll for this evening's escapade and, since you have experience in such matters, you must admit that my price is a small one.' Then he seemed to consider. 'It is either that, or you can tell me who you really are and what you were doing at that party.'

From the expression on his face, he probably thought she would lose her nerve and confess everything. She stared across the carriage at him, considering. The annoying thing about his demand was that it was not entirely unpleasant. She had been kissed before, of course, and found the whole experience rather tepid. But none of the previous gentlemen had been quite so handsome as this one, nor as daring.

And he was also right that tonight had been an adventure. Not a particularly pleasant one and she had no intention of repeating it. But shouldn't she gain something from it?

'If it makes a difference,' he added, 'I am going to the Horse Guards tomorrow to get orders that will send me back to Spain. There, I might die at any minute.' He gave a theatrical sigh. 'Yours might be the last kiss I ever receive.'

She could not help it. She smiled. 'How often have you told that to a woman?'

'More times than I can count,' he admitted.

'Is it often successful?'

'You would be surprised.' He blinked innocently, probably trying not to appear like the rogue he obviously was.

To his credit, it was working. He did deserve some sort of reward for rescuing them. And so did she for coming out on this fool's errand and risking her reputation for Felicity. If she was never to see him again, what harm could it do?

'Do you promise not to tell?'

He crossed his heart with a finger. 'On my honour, I will not tell a soul.'

'All right,' she said. 'I will kiss you.' Now she sounded ridiculously prim and not like the sophisticated woman she was claiming to be. He was laughing at her, she was sure, for he turned his head and offered his cheek, pointing to a spot to the left of his mouth, daring her to give him the only kiss he thought she had the nerve to.

This was the moment when she should con-

fess the truth and beg him to take her home.
But that would make her look like the foolish girl he thought she was and no better than
his cousin. The idea annoyed her. She was a
grown woman and she had a mind to prove
it to him.

She lunged.

It was better that she did not stop to think
for there were a hundred good reasons not
to. Otherwise, she'd never have the nerve to
do what she was doing, which was to launch
herself against him, knocking his body back
against the squabs, seizing his chin and turning his head so she could reach his mouth. It
was open, probably ready to tease her again,
so she stopped it with her own.

Claudine had explained the art of kissing
to her, more as a caution against what men
might wickedly attempt then as something
she might do for herself. But then, nice girls
never instigated kissing, much less thrust their
tongues into the mouths of sceptical gentlemen in carriages.

But perhaps it should happen more often.
This Will fellow seemed to be rather a cold
fish, or perhaps he was simply too shocked
to respond. But the kiss was still better than

any she had got from previous suitors. Those soft, passionless advances had left her fearing that there was something wrong with her own lack of response.

But clearly, the problem was not with her. This kiss, which she could control, left her tingling to the tips of her toes with unexpected power. And then the man under her seemed to wake from his stupor and it became even better. In response to her thrusting tongue, he pillaged her mouth as if he really thought he might die tomorrow and did not want to waste a moment. His tongue moved against hers, demanding an answer that she was eager to give.

The carriage lurched, throwing her against him, and he took the opportunity to spread his legs, cradling her body between his thighs so she could feel the hardening bulge of him pressing into her hip.

She pulled away from him then, breathing in air that smelled of rum and lust and did little to clear her head. But if her honour meant anything to her, she must remember that what she had done tonight was dangerous. If she did not stop things now, she might be trapped in the arms of a man who showed no mercy at her inexperience.

But why, now that it was happening, why was it exciting and not terrifying, as it should be? Why did she want even more from him?

As if he could sense what she wanted, he pulled her back and his kiss became wilder, his tongue meeting hers in a commanding thrust. Then his mouth was on her throat and his hands were on her breasts, palming and kneading through the fabric of her gown. It made her want to rip the cloth away and beg for his kisses, hot against her nipples, rough and forceful as he was on her mouth.

No! If anyone begged, it should be him. She pulled away again, slapping him smartly on the cheek and diving back to her side of the carriage.

He gave a moan of frustration and reached for her again.

'You said one kiss,' she reminded him with a firm smile. Then she glanced out the window to recognise a street not too far from her home. It would mean a half-mile run in the dark, but it would be worth it to get away before the fellow learned her true direction. So, she grabbed his stick and rapped on the wall to signal the driver to stop.

'Wait,' he said, reaching for her again. 'You can't leave me like this.'

'Can and will, Captain,' she said, blowing a last kiss into the darkness. Then she grabbed for the door, jumped down from the carriage and darted across the street and into the darkness before she could do anything else that she might regret tomorrow.

Chapter Three

$\sim\!\!\infty\!\!\sim$

After the disappearance of the mysterious girl, Will directed the carriage to return him to his house where he tried to sleep. He did not rest easy. But then, he never did any more. Between the pain in his arm and the war in his head, sleep was near impossible.

Or perhaps it was merely large, blue eyes, soft dark hair and full breasts that had rendered him sleepless. Who had she been? Not a courtesan, surely. She had been bold enough to kiss him, but there was a freshness about her, an innocent pleasure in the act that was nothing like the jaded caresses of a professional lover. It was the reason he was still thinking about the kiss, even as the empty hours passed.

He wondered what had happened to her.

She had kissed like an angel and then slapped sense into him and run for home. When the carriage had stopped, it had not been in front of any particular house, but the neighbourhood had been a nice one. She was probably the daughter of a noble who had been too afraid of scandal to give him her real name. He could not blame her. It had been foolish of her to go to James's club at all. She had been lucky enough to meet him there and not some scoundrel. But the relative innocence of their encounter would do nothing to save her reputation should word of it get out.

He sighed. She had to be an innocent to succumb to such a line as the one he had given her. In ten years of soldiering, how many last kisses had he got? And had any of them stuck in his heart as this one did? If ever there was a kiss worth dying on, this had been it.

If he wanted another, he should go to Felicity and ask the name of her friend. But there would be no point in it. She had only given in to him after knowing he would soon be gone. And he did mean to leave. He could not find his own peace without returning to finish the war he had been fighting. It was not fair to either of them to ask for more from this beautiful stranger than he had already received.

He waited until the sun was up, then shaved and dressed before going to the offices at the Horse Guards to settle the matter of his future with the army. Once there, he found himself standing at rigid attention while a major examined his medical records with a sigh. 'At ease, Captain,' his superior grumbled, not looking up from the papers.

'Thank you, sir,' he said, trying not to sigh with relief as he unlocked the joints of his bad arm. If he wanted to go back into battle, he did not dare show weakness now.

But it seemed that dissembling was not working. 'The fact that you are clearly in pain as we speak says much about your readiness, Grosvenor.'

'I am getting better every day,' he insisted. At least he thought he was. Sometimes, it seemed that he could not remember what it was like to be without pain.

'But the surgeon says there will be limits to your recovery.' The Major spared him a glance that probed like a lancet.

'The doctors are wrong,' Will said, keeping rigid control of voice and temper.

'In the meantime, there is much need of good men here in London,' the Major said, gesturing at the piles of papers on his desk. 'And there may be promotion and decoration for time already served,' he added.

'I do not want a promotion. I want to go back to the fight,' Will blurted out. 'All I need is a little time to heal.' What he needed was his command back. This enforced rest was the exact opposite of that. There was too much silence in it, too much time to think about things he'd rather not remember.

But instead of listening to his perfectly reasonable request, the Major reached behind his desk and produced his own sword, which was too bright and shiny to have ever seen battle. Then he unsheathed it and tossed it to Will.

He made a grab for it and watched in horror as his grip failed and the weapon clattered to the floor.

As he stooped to pick it up, the Major sighed again and said, 'I think you have your answer, Captain. At such time as you feel sufficiently recovered to man a desk, return here for your assignment. Until that time…?'

'Rest,' Will said in response. 'If that is all you have to say…'

'It is that or resign your commission,' the Major said and this time there was genuine regret in his voice. 'And now, Captain, if you will let yourself out, I have other matters to attend to.'

'Yes, sir,' he said, trying not to let the rising panic show on his face. If he could not go back to Spain, what was he to do with himself?

He brooded on the question most of the day and no answers were forthcoming. After the disappointment of the morning, it was no comfort to know that his evening would be spent facing down society at its most proper. At the ball he was now attending, there would be no high stakes gambling, excessive drinking, or rooms full of willing courtesans. There was not even the presence of his cousin Felicity, who had come down with a sudden megrim when she realised that he would be going along with the family.

She had nothing to fear from him for he would not dream of revealing her secret. But he hoped the worry over it would make her more cautious in the future.

'When you were on the Peninsula, you must have missed the English beauties we have here tonight.' From beside him, Freddie Fitzroy smiled out at the crowded floor where his own wife was currently dancing with another man. He'd met Freddie at Oxford and could not help liking the fellow who was the most gregarious member of the outgoing Fitzroy family. On his recent return to London, Will had discovered that Freddie had ignored the long-standing Claremont–Fitzroy feud and married Felicity's older sister, Dorothea.

The pair of them was the talk of the Season and were seen anywhere the smart set gathered. Since he seemed to love being out in society, Freddie must think that Will enjoyed it as well. But had he really missed any of this? He gazed out at the sea of fluttering fans and feathered turbans. The women before him resembled nothing as much as a flock of birds, loud, flighty and fragile.

He'd had enough of fragility, both his own and that of others. It was the first step down the road to uselessness. But his friend was awaiting an answer, so he gave him one. 'That just shows that you have not experienced the spell of a pair of fine, Spanish eyes.'

Freddie laughed in response, hinting that they could debate the details at a later date, when the company was not mixed.

So, his answer had been no answer at all and did nothing to solve the problem at hand. He was out in public and expected to make nice. But, if he was honest, his arm was aching and his nerves, which had been so steady in battle, were rattled by the noise and laughter around him. It did not matter to him one way or the other if some silly girl went without an escort because of his absence, he was going to go home.

Then the nearest circle of dancers turned and he saw *her* weaving through the patterns of the steps, her head thrown back in a laugh, exposing her elegant white throat, the same one he had buried his face in the night before. If he brushed away the powder on it, it was likely he would still find the marks of his kisses there, hidden in plain sight.

His loins tightened as he thought of the kiss she had given him, all but daring him to take his fill of her, and then her coy refusal after she'd raised his blood to the boiling point.

What would she do tonight when he introduced himself and offered her a dance?

His first impulse was to wade into the circle and drag her out, to demand an explanation, or another kiss, or both. But that was not how things were done in London, even if the woman was willing. He expected there would be flirting and simpering and pretence, all of it pointless since they both knew that, when the lights were low, she would be ready to go where he asked her to.

But all of it must begin with a proper introduction and Freddie owed him that for dragging him to this place. 'Who is that girl?' he said, pointing a finger in her direction and hoping it did not shake as he did so.

'My little sister?' His friend laughed. 'Surely you have met her before.'

Sister? Dear God in heaven, how could that force of nature be anyone's sister? If he gave any hint of what had happened between them, he would be dead before the sun rose.

'No, on my honour, I have not,' he said, probably too swiftly to seem innocently curious. But if it was truly the same girl, there was no way he could admit an acquaintance, or she would expect him to marry her immediately because of the dishonour he had done her.

'Then let me introduce you,' Freddie said with a laugh and grabbed his sister off the floor as the dance ended. 'Annie, come here and met one of my oldest friends.'

She was smiling at her brother, an expression full of mischief that raised Will's blood and his spirits. And then she turned to look at him and...

There was nothing there. No recognition at all. And for a moment, he was convinced that he had been mistaken. It could not have been her. Surely a kiss that had been as moving as the one that they shared would have left some trace on an innocent girl.

But now she was blinking at him, exquisitely polite and as oblivious to the turmoil he was in as if she'd been born yesterday.

'This is the Will Grosvenor I told you of, when I was away at school,' Freddie said, clapping Will on the back, and reaching to draw his sister closer.

'Freddie did not tell me that you had bought a commission,' she said with a welcoming smile. 'It is good to have you safely back in England.'

Actually, it was not good at all. He did not understand England any more. He certainly did not understand the women in it if the rest of them were anything like her. But he ignored his feelings and said, 'Thank you', trying to keep the confused stammer out of his voice.

'And I assume Freddie has told you of me as well?' she said, the rising inflection reminding him that she expected some sort of polite compliment in exchange.

'No,' he said, for he could think of nothing in previous conversations that had prepared him for such a meeting.

'No?' she said with a frosty smile, then turned and struck her brother with her fan in a playful rebuke. 'You did not speak of me at all? I am sad to be so quickly forgotten when I am out of your sight.' Then she looked back at William to give him another chance to make nice, 'Isn't he incorrigible?'

'It might not have been him at all. I probably just forgot,' he said and immediately realised that he had made another mistake. He should have said something glib to assure her that there was no way anyone could have forgotten such a charming girl. And, in truth, she was feeding him all the opportunities to flatter her. He just had to return them, like batting a tennis ball back over the net.

But it had been years since he had been in a ballroom and his society manners had always been lacking. If Ed were here, he would have had a response that would leave this girl hanging on his words and his arm. But Will could not think of anything to say beyond, 'I am sorry I mauled you last night, but you were the one who started it and you certainly enjoyed it at the time.'

Thank God, the interlude appeared to be over. She was giving her brother a mildly quizzical look, as if wondering why he had bothered to introduce a man so disinclined to speak. 'Well,' she said with a pitying look, 'it has been charming to meet you. But now you must excuse me. The next dance is beginning and my card is full.' It was a set down and one he most heartily deserved.

As she walked away, her brother let out an embarrassed laugh. 'Better luck next time, old friend. She did not mean to be rude, I'm sure. But she is the most popular girl in London and is used to having her pick of men.'

Even his best friend thought him unworthy of her. But how popular was she if she knew how to kiss like that? Did her brother know that she was frequenting James's establishment? He gave a shake of his head, thoroughly confused. Then he choked out what he should have when she was present. 'She seems a most charming girl. Your family must be very proud of her.'

'That we are,' her brother said, then directed him to the card room where he could lick his wounds in peace.

Annie smiled at her partner, the Duke of Penrith, forcing herself to laugh at his flirtatious comments as her mind reeled from this latest meeting with the Captain. When she had left him last night, it had not occurred to her that she might meet him again and so soon. He had promised that he was just be passing through London on the way to some posting or other. But apparently he had lied to her and here he was, with her brother, of all people.

Was there a chance that he didn't remember her? He had been quite drunk, after all. It had been dark, at the club and in the carriage, and she had been dressed as a servant with her dark hair in a simple bun instead of piled on her head and dressed in jewels and feathers.

That was a vain hope. No one could be so far gone as to miss the obvious truth. More likely he had been stunned to silence on finding that his friend's sister had attempted to kiss him senseless less than a day ago.

Fortunately, he had chosen to say just what she wanted, which was nothing at all. He had allowed her the luxury of pretending that they had never seen each other before and, hopefully, he had come away with the message that she never wanted to see him again.

At least, not in the way they had last night. It had been exciting, of course. Thrilling in the base sort of way that she had been warned against all her life. She could see why society frowned on such kissing, because even in circumstances that were less than ideal, she had wished to continue and might have given herself up to him had he persisted.

If he found that out, he would think she was as bad as the courtesan she had pretended to be. As it was, he might be trying right now to warn Freddie of her behaviour. Or maybe he was acting like the rest of those perfidious Claremonts and preparing to report the incident to the society editors of *The Times*. If anyone learned of it, she would surely earn the title of the Society's Most Scandalous on the tattle page at the end of the summer. It would be the death of her reputation.

But a part of her wondered if one kiss was really so bad. She looked around the room at the men who had danced with her thus far and tried to remember why it was that her reputation was important to her. It was important to them, certainly, for no one wanted a wife that could not be trusted to remain pure.

But why was there so little question as to what wives might want in return? She had spotted several of these fellows at the club last night, cavorting with all manner of loose women and drinking Montgomery James's claret even though he had attempted to ruin innocents like herself and Felicity.

Attendance at James's club was a black mark against the Captain as well. It was a good thing that he had no intention of courting her, or...

Or what? She certainly did not want to marry someone who counted Mr James as a friend. But if she meant to snub him in public as she had just now, what reason should she give? She could not exactly tell the family that she had already kissed him and enjoyed it too much.

It was all moot. She still did not know whether he intended to stay in London for the Season, or if he was even looking for a wife. For all she knew, he might already be married. That thought made her even angrier and she could not help shooting a dark look in his direction of the card room, as her partner danced her past it.

In any case, she was not about to allow herself to be courted by him or put herself in a position where she might be tempted to succumb to his charms. For the sake of her future, what had happened last night must never have happened. From now on, if she saw Captain William Grosvenor, she would be scrupulously polite and as proper as it was possible to be. Then, any doubts he had about her behaviour would be forgotten, along with their kiss.

Chapter Four

The next day, Will chanced on Freddie Fitzroy again and, as usual, he suggested a day
that was going to be good fun, beginning with
a trip to Gentleman Jackson's for some spar-
ring.

Will had been all for it. Boxing was a pale
imitation of actual battle, but it was easier to
take than this relentless peace.

It was only once he got there that he realised that he was no longer fit for even a
pretend battle. He could only hold his arm
in front of his face for a few moments and
when he did, blocking a blow was agonisingly
painful. His right fist was totally useless for
striking anyone. He felt as weak as a kitten
batting at a string.

All the same, he did his best to laugh it off

and to shout approval as his friend boxed, swallowing his jealousy and trying to believe that his present weakness was only a temporary thing. But he could not be sure of that. Not really. This recovery had gone on far too long, and improvements were coming far too slowly.

Perhaps he should take the opportunity, as presented by God, to make up for the incident in the carriage. If Freddie ever found out how Will had treated his sister, he would receive a lot more than a series of jabs and feints. So, he purposely dropped his guard and let some of the attacks in, taking a portion of the drubbing that he richly deserved. Perhaps it would knock some sense into his head and remove the desire to go looking for another kiss from Lady Anne Fitzroy.

But apparently not. After the sparring, Freddie wanted to stop at his father's town house to check on an estate matter, but promised drinks at the club immediately after. Will followed without objection, half hoping that he would see her again, but still unsure what he would say if he did. Was he supposed to apologise for something that had been none of his fault? Or was it up to her to be contrite? Maybe he would not have to find out.

Once at the Fitzroy house, Freddie pushed him in the direction of the salon to wait while he talked with his father. But as Will entered the room, he realised he was not alone. Lady Anne sat by the window, her knitting in her hand.

He turned to excuse himself again, but Freddie was there behind him, blocking the way. He grinned and gave him a gentle shove that sent him over the threshold. 'Just as I hoped. Last night's meeting did not go as you wished. Better luck today, Will. Annie, play nice.' And then he was gone, leaving the two of them alone.

Will stood, shifting uneasily on the threshold until the woman inside gave him a chilly smile and said, 'You might as well come in. Once he gets an idea into his head that I should meet someone, he will not let it go until we have at least spoken to each other.'

He stepped in and stared at the door, considering. After the kiss they'd shared, they definitely knew each other well enough to shut it. But the family did not know that and would think him beyond forward if he took that liberty. He might end up accidentally married if he attempted privacy too soon.

'Leave it open,' she said with a roll of her eyes. 'There is never anyone in this side of the house at this time of day anyway. We can speak freely.'

'Very well, Lady Anne,' he said and walked into the room to join her. He took a seat on a chair at a respectful distance from where she sat, then returned a smile much more respectful than the one she gave him. 'We meet again.'

'It was no doing of mine,' she assured him.

He nodded. 'Last night, I got the impression that you never wanted to see me again.'

'And the night before, you told me I would never see you again,' she said with a sigh.

'Things are not going as planned,' he said with an embarrassed shrug.

'For either of us,' she said, giving him a look that said he could go to Spain or the devil, for all she cared.

'Today was Freddie's doing, not mine,' he said, not entirely sure it was true. 'I think he is under the impression that we will suit.'

'Freddie is an idiot,' she said through gritted teeth.

Will touched his lips. 'You must admit, there is a certain compatibility. Between us.'

'I admit no such thing,' she said. 'When the incident occurred, I was under the impression that you wanted a final kiss before returning to Spain.'

'It was a goodbye kiss,' he said, smiling.

'And yet, here you are,' she said, then added, 'The kiss was supposed to be a diversion.'

'It certainly was that,' he agreed.

'So that I could get away without you following me,' she said, fuming.

'You had no reason to fear me,' he said. 'I'd have taken you home without question, had you been honest with me.'

'You were in that horrible place,' she said with a shudder. 'That alone made trusting you a questionable proposition.'

'You were there as well,' he reminded her. Then, he considered. 'And why were you there?'

She gave him a tortured look as if she wanted to speak, but did not know how.

'Let me guess,' he said with a sardonic grin. 'You were led astray by some gentleman who did not care for your reputation and thought that one visit to a gambling house would not make a difference. It was only when you arrived there that you realised how wrong you were.'

For a moment, her face darkened and her mouth opened, as if preparing to contradict him. Then it closed again and she muttered, 'Something like that.'

'Well, I trust you have learned your lesson,' he said, suddenly uneasy.

'Of course,' she said with a nod, looking not the least bit sincere.

Now he was really worried. He did not know much about women, but he was quite sure when they were as agreeable as this one was, they were likely up to no good. 'And, of course, the ki—' He glanced at the open door as a servant passed by and corrected himself. 'What happened after will never be mentioned again.'

'Thank you,' she said, not bothering to sound grateful. 'If any word of that escapade gets out, I run the risk of being named Society's Most Scandalous and neither of us wants that.'

'Whatever are you talking about?' he said with a frown.

'Society's Most Scandalous,' she said with

a look of amazement. 'Surely you have heard of it.'

'In truth, I have not,' he said, struggling to conceal his impatience.

'It is simply the most important competition of the Season,' she said. 'No young lady wants to win it, of course. It would be the ruin of them socially. But we all want to read who will be chosen and watch the gossip sheet for each hint.'

'Strangely enough, I did not have time to read the tattle sheets when I was in Spain,' he said and gave her a blank expression.

She gave a frustrated sigh. 'You are mocking me again.'

'I would never,' he said with an equally deadpan stare.

'It may not seem important to you, but it will be all the talk of the *ton* the day the announcement is made. The likes of Montgomery James compete to be considered, since it will cement the reputations they are trying to cultivate. But someone like you would never want a part in it.'

'And again, you mention this James,' he said with a shake of his head. 'You had best have nothing more to do with him, if you truly want to keep your name out of the scandal sheets.'

'My behaviour towards him has been within the bounds of propriety,' she said, giving him a firm smile.

'Except for the night I met you,' he reminded her.

'I did not even see him that night,' she said. 'Once I realised what sort of gathering it was, I went straight to the ladies' retiring room.'

'And mingled with courtesans,' he said, still disapproving.

'You were there as well,' she reminded him. 'Drunk and looking for trouble.'

'That is different,' he said with an air of superiority. 'I am a man.'

'It is grossly unfair,' she corrected. 'If women knew the way men were behaving at that gathering, they would want nothing to do with the lot of you.'

He shrugged. 'That is probably true. But it is the way of the world and you had best get used to it.' It was strange to see her so angry about his presence at the party. It was as if she somehow blamed him for the way things had gone that night. Perhaps she thought he only helped her because of Felicity and would have been a menace otherwise.

Or perhaps it was that a soldier was someone to be dallied with and then rejected. She was the daughter of a duke and destined for someone born to a title and lands, not a man who had to fight for his pay.

His brother would have suited her better. Of course, Ed was dead now and, like it or not, his house and fortune had come to Will. If he wanted to, he could cast the past aside and be the man she was looking for.

The idea was insane and he pushed it away. He was not his brother and never would be.

She blinked at him, waiting for him to say something, obviously unwilling to carry the conversation further. He could not exactly walk back into the hall and wait. After last night's display of interest, Freddie expected him to try to get to know his sister. But since it was clear she wanted nothing to do with him, how was he to go about it?

He cleared his throat, and the noise was embarrassingly loud in the room, a pompous harrumph that startled both of them. He began again. 'Enough of that, then. It will be some time before Freddie returns and he expects us to entertain ourselves. Let us forget the past and begin as if we have just met. So, Lady Anne, how are you enjoying your Season?'

She gave him a long sceptical look in response, then with a false smile and a voice perfectly suited for company, replied, 'I like it very well, thank you, Captain Grosvenor. And how are you enjoying your return to London?'

Not at all. And it was all the more miserable now that he must sit here in this dainty salon, sparring with a wilful female. Since she clearly wished him gone, it was proving to be more exhausting than his session at Gentleman Jackson's.

'Fine,' he said at last on a sigh. 'I like it well.'

'And your visit with your cousins?' she asked, her smile growing even more false. 'Felicity is about my age, I believe.'

She knew perfectly well how old Felicity was. She had only mentioned her to remind him that she was not alone at the party the other night. Had the two of them arrived at James's club together? If so, he could believe that this worldly girl had tricked his cousin into accompanying her.

'Felicity is well,' he replied, 'though I admit she is rather naive. I worry about the company she has fallen in with and do not mean to let them lead her astray.' Then he gave her a direct look so she might have no doubt whom he was referring to.

'I doubt you need to worry about that,' she said with an expression of obvious distaste. 'I have no intention of spending any more time than necessary with her or any other member of your family.'

In comparison to this, the rest of her snubs had been subtle. Apparently, he had goaded her to the point where she felt this blunt rejection was needed.

'I can ask for nothing more than that,' he said.

At that moment, Freddie appeared in the doorway and froze, staring at the pair of them in surprise. 'I am all done with Father and came to see how you two are getting on together.'

'Fine.' They said the single word in unison, but the tone she used did nothing to hide her animosity.

'I can see that,' Freddie, replied, with an exasperated expression. 'If you will excuse us, Sister, I will take the Captain somewhere he might receive better hospitality. France, perhaps.'

'Do as you wish,' she said with a shrug and picked up her knitting again with a dismissive shake.

'Good day then, Lady Anne,' Will said and left the room with hopes that he would be able to stay as far from her as she wished him to.

After the men had left her, Annie waited in silence until the count of ten, when she could be reasonably sure that they were out of earshot. Then she threw her knitting aside and pounded the brocade pillows of the couch until the rage in her subsided.

The nerve of the man. Had he come here specifically to lecture her on her outing to Montgomery James's party? He had evidently decided that what had happened was all her fault and that, somehow, she had led Felicity astray.

It was probably the kiss that had done it. She had behaved so brazenly when they were alone together that there was no way to explain that she had not been the instigator of the entire night. And she could not defend herself without defaming his foolish cousin.

It was a good thing that she had no desire to see him again. Because if, for example, she wanted another kiss like the one they had shared, there would be no way to get it now that she had promised to stay away from him.

'Annie!' She could hear her brother approaching, stomping down the corridor long before he arrived. It gave her the chance to compose herself, straighten the pillows and retrieve her knitting so she could be the picture of propriety by the time he arrived, fuming in the doorway.

'Yes?' she said with an innocent blink.

'What cause do you have to be so rude to my friend?' he asked, hands on hips.

'What cause do you have to foist him on me at every opportunity?' she responded.

'You are two of my favourite people and would be very well suited, once you get to know each other. In addition to that, Will is clearly smitten with you.'

'He most certainly is not,' she said, appalled at the idea.

'I beg to differ,' her brother said. 'When he first saw you, he looked as though he'd been poleaxed. What other explanation can there be?'

'I have no idea,' she said, trying not to flinch. 'But the feeling is not reciprocated.'

'And why is that?' he said, confused. 'What has the poor man done to you, other than to serve his country honourably and be excruciatingly polite to you, despite your rudeness? When I left him in the carriage just now, he did not say a word against you.'

'You, on the other hand, have no compunctions about blaming me,' she said.

'Because you are obviously at fault,' he said, shaking his head. 'It is the reason you are not successfully matched, even though the Season is almost over. You are too particular.'

'It is not unreasonable of me to want to marry for love, as the rest of the family has,' she said, annoyed.

'You will not find love if you do not open your mind to it,' he said. 'And the only thing you could possibly have against a man you have just met is his family connection to the Claremonts. As someone who married a member of that family, I take exception to your prejudice.'

'I do not dislike all members of the family,' she insisted. 'I have no complaint against Dorothea.'

'How magnanimous of you,' he said with a disgusted sigh. 'But that does not excuse your behaviour to Will. I expect the next time you see him that you will behave properly.'

There would be no next time. They had agreed to that between them. It was simply a matter of time before they persuaded Freddie to leave them alone.

Her brother was barely gone before her mother hurried into the room and sat down next to her with a worried expression. 'I have just heard the most scandalous thing,' she said, but if it was gossip, she showed no joy in sharing it.

'What concerns you?' Annie replied, putting down her knitting to listen.

'That horrible Montgomery James has been talking to all the young ladies of the Season, trying to convince them to go to his club to gamble.'

'Really,' Annie said, glad that her mother had no idea what she'd got up to.

'He is only doing it to see the ruin of some innocent young lady for his own amusement,' she said with a sorry shake of her head.

'I suspect that is true,' Annie replied. 'Or he might be vying for the title of Society's Most Scandalous.' She reached for her knitting again, hoping that the conversation could be at an end.

'Well, he certainly deserves it. If you see him, you are not to talk to him,' she said firmly.

'That will be rather difficult, Mother,' Annie said as carefully as possible. 'The man is invited everywhere. I cannot cut him without making people wonder at my reason for it and making the connection between us even stronger.'

'I suppose that is true,' her mother said with a sigh. 'I doubt we would see him at all if he did not have the ear of the Prince Regent. It has made him into a darling of the *ton*, but it brings the quality of any gathering down to have him there.'

Annie gave what she hoped was a final, ambivalent nod and went back to her work.

'And you must remember that talking to the likes of him gets you no closer to making the match that you eventually will,' her mother said with a critical nod.

'And who would that be with?' Annie replied, setting her work aside again with a sigh.

'I had hopes that you would be able to tell me,' her mother said with a hopeful smile. 'Have you really found no one who interests you? Because now that Freddie and Hattie and Kitty are all married...'

'I am the only one left,' Annie said glumly.

'It is not that we regret having you with us another year,' her mother said. 'But weddings are so delightful and I would not mind having another one to finish off the Season.'

'And do you have any suggestion as to whom the groom might be?' Annie asked with another sigh. 'Because, truly, I have no idea.'

'Not a one?' her mother said, surprised. 'You seem very popular with all the gentlemen and several of them have spoken to your father about offering for you.'

'And none of them has been given any real encouragement by me,' she said quickly. 'I have flirted, of course. I am equally polite to all of them. But none of them has made me feel...'

Well, almost none. But she could hardly call what she had been to Captain Grosvenor polite or flirtatious. The night they had met, she had been desperate to get away and that had likely added something to the interaction.

'You think you have not met the right man for you,' her mother said with a wise nod. 'But you must give the ones around you a fair chance. Love does not always happen in an instant. Sometimes it grows slowly, like a plant, and takes over the garden of affection before you know it.'

'What you are describing is called a weed,' Annie said, stifling a smile.

Her mother gave her an innocent shrug. 'Not all men are perfect when you find them. Some need a bit of pruning. All I wish to say is that you give the ones around you a fair chance before rejecting them.'

'And sometimes, weeds are simply weeds,' Annie said, thinking of the Captain. 'But I will do my best to be fair. All the same, do not be surprised if you are giving me this same advice at the beginning of next year.'

Chapter Five

That night, as Annie prepared to go out, she did her best to put her family's advice behind her. The evening would be just another ball, she reminded herself, adjusting the brooch that held her turban in place. The same people would be there as were always there and she would treat them as she always had.

Perhaps that was the problem with it. After months of going around in society, yet another dance with the same people, sharing the same gossip and eating the same food seemed like an empty exercise. She wanted something new, something different.

It almost made her wish that she had not met the Captain under such unfortunate circumstances, since he was the only fresh face in London. He would have stories that no one had heard, fresh gossip and a new perspective on what others were doing.

She thought for a moment, then stifled a laugh at her own foolishness. There was not a person in her acquaintance less likely to gossip than the tight-lipped Captain William Grosvenor. It was just as well since she did not want him tattling about her trip to Mr James's club.

All the same, she wished that he had the sort of social skills that would make him a sparkling dinner companion. Then, perhaps, she could at least pretend to do what Freddie expected of her and socialise with the man before rejecting him. But it seemed he could not stop being pompous and critical, even for a moment.

Since she did not want to see him again, when she finally arrived at the ball, he was the first person she saw. He was standing on the other side of the room from her, looking stiff, awkward and miserable, albeit as handsome as ever. It was his bright red coat and polished boots that made him stand out from the crowd, she was sure. That and his height.

Of course, there were other tall men here

and other soldiers as well. But there was something about the Captain that was different from other men. Perhaps it was because he had seen battle. He seemed more solid and real than the rest of the crowd. Freddie had mentioned that he was injured, but she could not see a difference in his movements other than a slight stiffness on his right side. Was it a brush with death that left him so sombre?

Whatever it was, it combined to make him a poor fit for this evening's crowd, which seemed even more light-hearted than usual. The champagne tonight was flowing freely and those who were not dancing were laughing and chatting without a care in the world.

Only the Captain was frowning. Perhaps she should go over and tease him, to make him even more uncomfortable.

Then she remembered her plan was to ignore Freddie's demands and stay as far away from the Captain as possible, so she remained where she was.

'Lady Anne.' Montgomery James was now at her side, bending low over her hand and planting a kiss on the air above her knuckles.

Even though there was no contact, she could feel the heat of his breath through her glove and she had to force herself not to shudder. She was not about to let him know that his attentions bothered her, or he'd likely try all the harder to annoy her. 'Mr James,' she said in a carefully modulated tone that gave neither too much approval nor disapproval.

'I missed you at my party the other night.'

Good.

The last thing she needed was his announcing, either here or in private, that he had seen her in such a place. She suspected that he had known all along what the party would be like and had tried to lure her there with the intent of ruining her.

'I was otherwise engaged,' she said with a shrug.

'Perhaps another time,' he said, looking up at her with a wolfish expression.

'You must send an invitation to my mother,' she said, giving him a naive blink and a dim smile. 'I am sure if your parties are as good as you claim that the entire family would like to come. It will be great fun.'

She was pleased to see him give a slight choke at the suggestion that she bring her parents. Then he regained control and his smile returned. 'If not that, then perhaps a carriage ride for just the two of us. I know a lovely and secluded road in the country.'

'I will have to ask my mother when I am free,' she said, dodging the invitation again. 'Or you can come to our musicale on Saturday. You can see me there and hear me sing.'

She saw him wince inwardly at the thought of an evening of tepid lemonade and equally tepid sopranos. 'I fear I am busy that night.'

'How unfortunate,' she said, relieved.

'I will have to settle for a dance tonight, then,' he said, holding out a hand for her dance card. He chose a waltz, of course, the most intimate dance of the night. It was not too troublesome because she had danced with him before and could at least count on the fact that he could keep the beat and avoid stepping on her toes. But she was sure she would hear from her mother later about the risks of associating with him.

As soon as James had passed on to the other side of the room, the Captain appeared beside her, looking down at her with such annoying intensity that she took a step back in alarm.

'What have I done now?' she said. 'Surely something wrong for you appear to be about to dress me down over it. Out with it now. What is the matter?'

He did not bother to answer, just continued to stare at her with the sternest of looks. Then he said, 'Might I have a turn around the veranda with you, Lady Anne?'

If he was just going to lecture her about something, it was the last thing she wanted. Even worse was the annoying thrill she felt at the idea that they might be alone again. It was best to refuse. 'I do not want to miss the next dance,' she said, glancing at the orchestra who seemed to be packing their instruments for a break.

He reached down and snatched her dance card, which was attached to her wrist on a ribbon, pulling it up to examine it. He raised one eyebrow at the blank space for the next dance, then grabbed the attached pencil and scribbled his name in the spot.

'Now you will miss nothing,' he said. Then he came to her side and held out his arm to her, with a significant stare.

This was the moment she should snub him, turn and refuse the offer and publicly embarrass him. But he had far too much power over her to risk doing that, so she timidly accepted his arm and allowed him to lead her out of the ballroom and into the night air.

A few other couples were gathered there, staring out at the gardens, or at each other, oblivious to the presence of any but themselves. If he wished a word alone without being overheard, it was as good a place as any. But he remained silent, letting the empty air wear on her nerves.

'Really, Captain,' she said with a coy smile. 'Are you going to speak, or just stare at me? If the latter, we could have just as easily remained in the ballroom. If you want a word with me, then go to,' she said with an expansive wave of her hand.

'How could you flirt with that man?' he said, clearly trying to contain a shudder of revulsion.

'What man are you referring to?' she said with a flutter of her fan. 'There have been so many this Season I hardly know how to count them.'

'You know perfectly well to whom I am referring,' he said through clenched teeth. 'Montgomery James.'

'I am not flirting with him,' she said. 'He is flirting with me and I am answering him.

We have been flirting all Season and nothing has come of it. I have no trouble countering his advances.'

'Says the woman who was at one of his parties and needed to be rescued by me to prevent her disgrace,' he added with a huff.

'The only reason I was there...' she said and then stopped. The truth did not reflect very well on his cousin. Perhaps she should not speak.

'Please, enlighten me,' he said. 'I assume that you wanted to test the boundaries of what society would allow you. Did you learn anything by it?'

He seemed decided to think the worst of her and there was little point in changing his mind. So, she gave a contrite bob of her head. 'It will not happen again.'

'It will if you continue to associate with James,' he said, giving her a dark look. 'How long with it take for you to succumb to his charms?'

'Succumb to his charms?' At this she could not help but laugh. 'He is the least charming man I know.'

'And yet you went to his club,' he said.

'Remember when you said that we would

not speak of that again,' she said, giving him a dark look, 'because I distinctly recall you making such a promise.'

'I only bring it up tonight because you gave me cause,' he said. 'I am trying to protect you.'

'I do not need your help,' she said, then added, 'Not any more, at least.'

The look he gave her made her feel helpless and foolish. But she was not going to change her behaviour based on the suggestions of one infuriating man.

She did her best to straighten her spine and give him an intimidating glare, failing miserably because it was clear from one look at him that he had seen things in his life so horrific that nothing in London would cow him to silence.

'I will take your helpful words under advisement,' she said, trying not to roll her eyes.

'See that you do,' he said. 'I do not want to have to save you twice.'

'Do not worry,' she said, annoyed. 'You and I will not cross paths again, if you can manage to leave me alone in the future.'

'I leave you alone?' he said with a sharp laugh.

'You are the one who keeps seeking me out,' she reminded him.

'The last visit was none of my doing,' he said hurriedly. 'Your brother arranged it. He thinks you owe me an apology, by the way.'

'Then I apologise,' she said hurriedly and made to go around him to go back to the ball-room.

'And what are you apologising for?' he asked, turning to block her way.

'For not treating you as I treat other gentlemen,' she said.

'Since you seem all too free with the other gentlemen here, it is probably for the best,' he said.

'I certainly do not,' she snapped, surprised. 'My behaviour is thoroughly proper at all times.'

He gave her a dark look.

'Almost all times,' she amended, remembering the party. 'But Freddie has noticed that I do not flirt with you, of all people.' She frowned, wondering if it was really so obvious that there was something different between them. 'He is of the impression that I dislike you simply because you are part of the Claremont family.'

'When actually you dislike me for other reasons entirely,' he finished for her.

'I do not dislike you,' she said hurriedly. It was not exactly a lie. She disliked how they had met and disliked her reaction to him. And she was not overly fond of the way he treated her, as if he had a say over her behaviour. But other than that…

He gave her a wry smile. 'Then you have a very generous spirit. I have done nothing to make myself particularly likeable. And on our first meeting, I did little to endear myself to you. Under other circumstances, things might have been quite different between us.'

She gave him a doubtful look. It was possible that, with time, he would not seem so overbearing and would listen to her long enough to see that she was not some cloth-witted female who could not manage her own life without help from a man. Anything was possible. But some things were highly unlikely.

Then he gave a huff of frustration and pulled her behind a potted palm to prevent anyone from hearing their conversation. 'The thing is, I do not dislike you. I simply cannot stand to see you running back into danger at the first opportunity presented. I swear, any soldier under my command would have better sense than to take such risks.'

'I am not a soldier under your command,' she snapped. 'And this is not Spain, nor is Mr James as clever as Napoleon. Despite what you think, I am quite capable of navigating a ballroom without courting disgrace.'

'That is not saying much,' he whispered.

'You give me too little credit,' she said with a shake of her head. 'My own brother is not as worried about me as you are.'

'Freddie does not have half an idea what you get up to, I am sure,' he replied, taking her by the shoulders.

'Unhand me this instant, sir,' she said with a hiss.

For a moment, he seemed surprised by the request, as if he had not realised that he was touching her. He looked down at his hands on her shoulders and then into her eyes.

And that was a mistake for both of them, she was sure. His eyes were amazingly dark. Why had she not noticed them before? The irises were a deep blue, almost engulfed by the pupils. She could lose herself in them, or perhaps she was finding herself. A moment later, when his lips touched hers, it was as if she had been searching for this place, this moment and this man all her life.

His hands stroked down her shoulders until they could catch her hands, holding them tenderly in his. But she could still remember what he might do with those hands, if they were alone and could not be interrupted at any moment.

And then it was over and he was looking guiltily around him, to make sure that no one had noticed their indiscretion.

'I am sorry,' he whispered, stepping away from her. 'I do not know what came over me.'

The same thing that came over her, she was sure. But to admit her feelings gave this stranger more power over her than she wanted him to have.

'See that it does not happen again,' she said, snapping her fan closed in a gesture of dismissal. Then she walked past him to return to the ballroom alone.

Will took a deep breath of the cool, night air and sank back into the darkness, banging his head slowly against the stone wall behind him. What had he been thinking to bring her out here into the night? More importantly, why had he kissed her again?

The answer to the last question was obvious. He had learned in the carriage that she was a very kissable woman. Those lips deserved to be enjoyed by a man, sipped from like fine wine and guzzled like fresh water.

But not by him. He was going back to the war as soon as he was able. He had no intention of taking a wife with him when he left. But neither was he going to leave her to the attentions of Montgomery James.

When he had been on the Peninsula, there had been an assumption, at the back of his mind, that there was an England he was fighting to preserve. A civility that was absent from the fog of war, filled with balls and tea parties, and women as ephemeral as spun sugar who married men like his brother, men with inherited wealth that knew from their first breath that they would never have to work for anything in their lives.

Ed had proved how ephemeral it all was by dying of consumption. He had always been the delicate one and, though it was painful, it was no real surprise that he was gone before his time.

And then there were men like himself, born without means and suited to a life of slashing and hacking through the blood and muck of battle and ill prepared to interact with the very thing that soldiers were supposed to preserve.

Lady Anne, with her perfectly puffed sleeves and her crisp ruffles, should not be able to withstand a drop of rain, much less the touch of a man. She belonged on a sofa in a parlour, to be admired from a distance and remembered as an ideal of what one might want, but did not dare to have.

It made the memory of the moment they'd shared all the more confusing. He'd found her where no lady should be and she'd kissed him like a woman and not a girl. Those lips could wake the dead. They had certainly woken him, body and soul.

But it had been one night and one kiss and he had not expected it to happen again. Why he had pulled her from the ballroom tonight was a more complicated problem. He had seen her with James and the response in him had been primal. Of all the men in the room, this was the one who could not have her, thus he was the only one she seemed to gravitate towards.

Was she doing it to make him jealous? Did she notice him at all? And why did it matter? If he wanted to attract any woman, it would not be the sort who seemed to thrive on the bustle of London, the parties and balls, the gossip and chatter. Even if he did something as foolish as offer for her, the answer would likely be a resounding no.

Suddenly, someone laughed in the darkness, the sound as sharp as a gunshot and he was back in Spain, dodging bullets and fighting for his life. He closed his eyes, then opened them again, staring off into the darkness to ground himself in the strange reality that was the London Season.

God, he needed a drink. And not the tepid champagne that this party offered.

He did not bother to bid farewell to his hostess, but stepped off the veranda and into the garden to walk to the front of the house and find his way home.

Chapter Six

Annie straightened her skirts and adjusted her grip on the book she held as she mounted the steps to the dirty brick building in front of her. St Michael's Soldiers' Hospital was a grim place where men of no particular class ended up when they were in no condition to afford the better, private homes where officers and gentry might recover from their wounds.

Though her mother had suggested she bring a Bible to read for the edification of the men there, she'd found that popular novels went over much better. A good yarn cut through the miasma of despair that hung over the place and over the men, who often had problems that could not be cured by a quick prayer from a rich stranger doing an hour or two of charity work.

As she worked her way down the ward, reading and writing letters for illiterate soldiers, she tried not to worry about the beds that had been full last week and were now empty. Hopefully, the men in them had recovered and found their way back to loved ones and not simply out on to the streets to beg.

But it was a relief to see one of her favourite patients still here and doing better. Sergeant Barnes was sitting up in bed, with the blankets bunched in his lap to disguise the stump of his missing leg. But judging by his colour, his other injuries were healing well. He looked better than she had ever seen him.

'Sergeant,' she said with a smile and a lady-like salute. 'How are you doing today?'

'My toes itch,' he said with a grin and hunched as if trying to bow without standing up. 'But I would have to go back to Alava to give them a scratchin' so there is little to be done.'

'You will not be here much longer, I think,' she said with an approving nod. 'You are looking a million times better than you did last week.'

He nodded back. 'They have given me

crutches to practise walking and, when I heal properly, I will get a peg.'

'That is good to hear,' she said, honestly relieved. If there was any chance of a future for this man, mobility would be important. 'And have you given thought to what you will do when you leave here? Do you have family to take you in, or are you on your own?'

'My Captain has a manor house and has offered me a job there as a groom.' He looked off into the distance, remembering better times. 'When I was on the farm, as a lad, I always liked working with the horses. They was big draught horses, of course, only fit for pulling a plough. It will be nice to handle the sort of fine horseflesh that gentlemen have.'

She smiled. 'It is good to hear you so happy about what is to come.' Other men were not so lucky, but Barnes, at least, had a reason to hope. 'Was this the same Captain you have been telling me about? The one that arranged for your stay here?'

'None other,' he said with a grin. 'And a finer man never lived. When we were on the Peninsula, he treated us like family. Never left a man behind and saw to it, when we were injured, that we had a place to go. And those that did not make it?' He paused for a respectful moment of silence. 'Well, he wrote letters to every mother and sweetheart, to assure them that their men died a good death. Many's the day I seen him crying his own tears over those letters, for he felt every loss like it was family.'

'He sounds like a very fine man,' she said, wondering why some soldiers she knew could not have such tender feelings. Then, the Sergeant settled back into his pillow and she picked up her book and began to read aloud.

Two hours later, after she had reached the end of the ward and said farewell to the patients, she was ready to spend the rest of the day running her own errands.

First, there was a trip to the modiste for a fitting of her newest ballgown and then a visit to a milliner for a bonnet, which required other stops for ribbons, gloves and a painted fan.

While she was walking down Bond Street on her way to her carriage, followed by a trail of footmen carrying her purchases, she spied Captain Grosvenor heading towards her less than a street away.

After the previous night's interaction, she was not sure it was wise to see him again. She did not want him to get the idea that she approved of clandestine kissing, since it was dangerously close to becoming a habit between them.

But it was too late to pretend that she hadn't noticed him. To cross the street would be an obvious snub and might call more attention than speaking to him. So, she forced a polite smile and looked him directly in the eye as he approached. 'Captain Grosvenor.'

'Lady Anne,' he said in a painfully formal voice and offered a crisp bow. 'Shopping, I see.' But the courtesy did nothing to soften the fact that he was looking at her stack of packages in disapproval, as if there was something unusual about a woman spending the day buying fripperies.

'That is why one normally comes to this neighbourhood. And what are you doing here?' she asked him, ready to be equally critical.

'I paid a visit to my tailor,' he said.

'And likely your bootmaker,' she said, admiring the shine on his Hessians. 'So, you are shopping as well.'

'Not as such,' he allowed.

'I understand,' she said, pretending to believe him. 'Purchasing clothing is much different when men do it.'

'We do not do it as often as you,' he said with a raised eyebrow. 'When I was in Spain, I was able to go months at a time without the need for a new hat.' Now he stared at her bonnet in distaste.

'By the look you are giving me, I need to shop again just to replace the hat I am wearing,' she said.

'I have no opinion about it,' he said, still not smiling.

'All the more reason for me to buy another,' she said. 'The correct response is to tell me that it is fetching, then to add that, of course, it is not as lovely as I am.'

'Since you have complimented yourself, it is hardly necessary for me to do so,' he said, looking as pompous and stiff as ever.

'Captain Grosvenor,' she said, tipping her head to the side. 'Was there a time, before the war, when you went about in society like a normal man?'

'Are you implying that there is something abnormal about my behaviour now?' he said.

'I simply wonder if you are like this with all women, or if there is something about me personally that you dislike.' she said.

'I do not dislike you,' he insisted. 'You are just too...' He made a strange gesture, evidently meant to indicate the quality that she seemed to possess in excess, which he could not manage to even name.

'Whatever this is,' she said, waving her arms back at him, 'I am sure it is not as bad as you make it out. No one else this Season has had a problem with it.'

'I imagine they do not, since they are soft, foolish and easily distracted by glamour.'

'Is that what you think of me?' she said, quietly outraged.

He was supposed to say no and set her fears to rest. Instead, he glanced around him and said, 'You are well suited to your surroundings.'

'You mean fit for shopping and not much else,' she said with a shocked laugh. 'When you are in London for a while, you will learn that there is nothing so objectionable in dressing up and dancing.' She looked at him closely. 'Unless, of course, you cannot dance well.'

She saw his expression darken and continued, 'That is it, isn't it? You are a poor dancer.'

'That has nothing to do with it,' he said, embarrassed.

'It would explain a lot,' she said, staring at him thoughtfully. 'If you are bad at the things that socialising requires, I could see why you would deem them lesser. But they are pleasures that many other people treasure. If you see no value in them, you might just as well stay home.'

'Perhaps I shall,' he said. 'But I receive so many invitations, it seems rude to discard them all.'

'So, you go about for the sake of your hostesses,' she said with a mocking sigh. 'If that is true, then you will find yourself married off to a girl just as foolish as I am by the end of the Season. Next time you receive an invitation, take the time to discover whether the hostess has a daughter of marriageable age.'

'They have been inviting me to…?' He gave another baffling gesture and it was accompanied by a look so shocked that she had to stifle a laugh. 'But I do not plan on getting married.'

Captain Grosvenor might have been quite

successful on the battlefield, but on the marriage mart he was green as grass. 'If you look around, you will see that single men are at a premium,' she explained gently. 'And since you are a handsome man with a decent fortune…'

'But my brother only just died,' he said surprised. 'I inherited the house, of course, but I told no one about the money.'

'You do not need to. Everyone knew Edward Grosvenor and had formed a good opinion of both his character and his finances. You are his heir, so it is assumed you will be much the same.'

'I am not the man my brother was,' he insisted. 'As soon as I am able, I am going back to Spain.'

'The mothers of the *ton* do not give a fig for your plans,' she said with gentle insistence. 'While you might go to the Peninsula, your house and money will be staying here. They can tell by your tailor what you can afford and the patronesses at Almack's know even more about your family's worth. If they have declared to their coterie that you are fair game, then the hunt is on.'

'It is a wonder we do not employ more

women spies,' he said, giving a slight shudder. 'They are too efficient at spiriting out what they want to know.'

'It is because men are too stubborn to admit that we have brains,' she said, looking him up and down again. 'I would not bother to announce my lack of marital plans if I were you. It only encourages women to try harder.'

'Women try too hard as it is,' he said with a frown that seemed to be directed at her. 'All the frills and ribbons... The constant parties and the endless dancing and flirting when they could look as they are and say what they mean...'

'I think you are being unnecessarily hard on them,' she said, meeting his gaze as if daring him to find fault. 'You are trying to apply the rules of war to London where we are fighting a battle of a different sort.'

'And what is that?' he said.

'We are trying to capture husbands,' she said, suddenly embarrassed to admit what everyone knew was the truth. 'And cannot do it wearing the same gown for months at a time. There is no advantage to economising when one is trying to attract attention with one's appearance. It is not as if the other men here wonder how long we can march without stopping or how quickly we can load a rifle. They want us to be able to dance and sing and be what you deem a useless decoration.'

'You are not useless,' he said with a pause that belied the truth of the statement. 'It is just that since I am not seeking a wife, I have trouble seeing the point in such preparations.'

'Fine,' she said, in a tone that should have warned him it was anything but. 'Then I see no point in changing my behaviour to please you. You have already made it clear that you have no interest in marriage. It is a good thing, for if you'd have asked me the answer would certainly be no.'

Then, she huffed off down the street, leading her train of overburdened footmen.

He stared after her, confused.

Since it had not been his intention to propose to her, it was a surprise to know that he had been refused. On one hand, he should never have mentioned marriage, since he had just met the girl and was not looking for a wife.

On the other, he had kissed her twice and it was possible that she had been anticipating a proposal. How many kisses was one allowed to steal from a lady before one was beholden to her?

If he was to ask her brother, the answer would probably be none. He would be halfway down the aisle before he could complete the question.

Thoughts of marriage aside, she was right about his ill treatment of her. There was nothing particularly unusual about her behaviour when he compared it with the women around her.

But then, none of the other women he'd met in London had kissed him as if their lives depended on his happiness. For a moment, when she was in his arms, he'd felt alive in a way he had not since Spain, before the final attack, when everything had been going his way. He'd held her and felt good and strong, not old and broken. The blood had surged in him and with it desire and passion.

He wanted it to mean something. And there was no way he could see that a kiss from such a woman as he'd met at the parties and balls that she seemed to revel in could mean anything beyond an aberration from her normal behaviour. She had proved him right with the speed with which she'd wanted to bury the act, to forget it for ever.

There was no way he could think to demand that she be more than she was. She owed him nothing. And yet he wanted so much more from her. He wanted her to be the girl in the carriage again, wild and uninhibited. He had wanted a second kiss and now he wanted a third.

He should be visiting James's club again for the courtesans, or asking Freddie and George about accommodating widows who might want to spend time with a lonely soldier who was not quite himself.

Or he could have the sense to avoid ladies altogether and go talk to someone who really understood what he was going through.

St Michael's Hospital gave him one more reason to miss the Peninsula. In the places he was used to seeing them, the sick and injured were kept in tents. Though the flies could be bad, the air was fresh and the outside only a few paces away.

Here, in the wards, the floors were dirty and the breeze from the windows carried only a few feet into the stuffy rooms, leaving the patients there tossing restlessly on their cots and longing for the breezes of Spain.

Despite that, the first soldier he met greeted him with a smile, his eyes squinted in mirth. 'Good day to you, Captain.'

'And to you, Sergeant Barnes,' he said in reply, after glancing at the chart at the foot of the man's bed to assure himself that the fellow was gaining strength.

'Pardon my lack of parade posture,' the Sergeant said, pulling himself up on his bed and snapping a weak salute.

His own shoulder twinged in response as he gave an answering gesture, then remarked, 'We are both too far from the front to worry about formality, Barnes. How are you feeling?'

'Worlds better,' the man said with a grin. 'The stump is heeling. No sign of infection. I will be up and around in a week or two, ready for duty.'

'Take your time, Barnes. The position in my stables will wait until you are ready for it.'

'And how is the arm?' the Sergeant said, giving him a critical look.

'Stiff,' Will admitted, seeing no reason to hide the truth. 'The surgeons let me keep it, but sometimes I wonder why. What good is it if it will not hold a sword?'

'You can still hold a woman with it,' the Sergeant reminded him, bringing back his earlier worries. 'And I had the sweetest one here just a few hours ago.'

'And where did you find one of those is a place like this, you old rogue?' Will said, grinning back at him.

Barnes sighed. 'Ah, my sweet little Annie is one of the angels of mercy that come to read to us and write our letters home.'

'A do-gooder,' Will said with a disappointed sigh. 'Come to convert you bunch of heathens, no doubt. Tell me, was it sermons or psalms you got out of her?'

'*The Castle of Otranto,*' he corrected. 'It is a ripping good story and she says she knows that men prefer it to being preached at when they are short of temper and limbs.'

'That is exceptionally wise of her,' Will said.

'She has the voice of an angel,' Barnes said with a sigh. 'And a face to match. She is the only thing I will miss about this place when I am gone.'

'I stand corrected,' Will said, impressed.

'It is a shame that more young ladies around here don't live up to her example.'

'Don't tell me you have been disappointed by the women of London,' the Sergeant scoffed. 'I was told a straight back and a fine uniform would win all the hearts when they wanted me to take the King's shilling.'

'The ladies I meet look fine enough,' Will admitted, 'but are nothing but damp squibs when you get to know them.' Or was it the opposite? Lady Anne had certainly seemed like a firecracker when he'd met her. But it had been an illusion, he was sure.

'Give it time, sir,' Barnes said with a nod. 'You will find someone worthy of you.'

'In Spain, perhaps,' Will said. 'Or when we march through France.'

'You mean to go back?' Barnes said, surprised.

'Do I have a choice?' Will said, setting his shoulders and ignoring the ache in the one of them.

'I would hope so,' Barnes said. 'I thank you for rescuing me, of course. But it was a narrow squeak for both of us. The best thing about that last attack was that it was bad enough to keep me out of the war for good and all.'

'But the rest were not so lucky,' Will said, feeling a fresh surge of the guilt that was always with him.

'And your returning to Spain will not bring a one of them back,' Barnes said bluntly.

'But there must be something I can do to make up for it,' Will said, trying not to sound as desperate as he felt when he thought of his final day of war.

'Do you mean to go back and kill as many as you lost?' Barnes said with a shake of his head. 'Because you have certainly done that already. You had your share of winning skirmishes before the end, you know.'

'I know,' Will said, trying not to think of all the men he had killed in service of England. 'But the war is not over. And I—'

'You are still alive,' Barnes said cutting right to the problem. 'And that is a good thing, you know.' Then, Barnes gave him a closer look. 'You do know that, don't you? Because, Captain, there is nothing more dangerous for a man in uniform then an officer who wants to die gloriously.'

'I do not want glory,' Will insisted. 'I want justice.' It was not fair that he had lived, when so many around him had died. He owed it to them not to give up. He had to make their deaths mean something.

'If you want justice, then you had best stay here and be a lawyer,' Barnes said, shaking his head. 'Because there was nothing fair in the war that I remember.' The Sergeant eased back into his pillows with a tired sigh. 'Now, tell me more about these horses that need caring for. Because no one shoots at a stable hand and that is what I want to be.'

Horses.

He had not forgotten the job he'd told Barnes he could have after the war. They'd both been near death that day and it had been a very important conversation. Talk of the future had kept them both going until they were safely back at camp.

He had simply forgotten to get the animals that would make it necessary to hire an extra groom.

But that could change. He certainly had the money for it. And if he could not bring back the dead, at least he could do some good in the life of one of the survivors. So as the Sergeant relaxed, Will told him of the horses he still had to buy.

Chapter Seven

Annie stood before the cheval glass in her room, staring at the gown she had just purchased, picking at the ribbons that held the sleeves in place. 'I do not like it. But I cannot think what is wrong with it.'

'There is nothing wrong with it,' her twin, Hattie, said, not looking up from her place on the edge of the bed. She was flipping idly through the pages of a novel and paying no attention to Annie's very real problems with her wardrobe.

'Since you have been married, I've had no one to give me an honest opinion on things.'

'Or to borrow gowns from when you get in moods like this,' Hattie added, with a smile.

'It is just wrong,' Annie said, shaking her head. If he thought her superficial, ribbons and lace would do nothing to convince him otherwise. 'I look like a bonbon.'

'Very sweet,' Hattie agreed.

Annie moaned. 'But I am not sweet. At least, I hope not.'

'Do you want to be bitter?' Hattie said with surprise.

'Worldly,' Annie suggested.

'Ahh,' Hattie replied. 'This is about a man, then.'

'It certainly is not,' Annie said hastily, untying a bow and letting the sleeve droop. His attitude should not annoy her as much as it did, for she did not normally care what people thought of her. She was who she was and she was quite satisfied with it.

Until today. For some foolish reason, the Captain's opinion of her mattered. There was something about the way he looked at her, as if he could strip away the decoration and see to her very soul, that made her want to impress him with her value.

'Who is he?' Hattie asked, not fooled.

'No one,' she replied.

'Not Montgomery James,' Hattie suggested.

'Ugh,' Annie said, reaching for some scissors to snip away some lace.

Hattie rose with a sigh and came to her, taking the scissors away. 'Stop before you ruin it. If you must change it, let Claudine. And I was wondering, since you said "worldly"...'

'James is a rake. I am not interested in his particular world,' she replied, wondering if some rumour of her escapade had escaped and come back to the family.

'That is good to know,' her sister replied. 'But then, who? Is it that Captain Grosvenor?'

'You know him?' she said, surprised.

'I have heard all about him,' Hattie said. 'And you as well.'

'What about me?' she demanded. 'And what does that have to do with him?'

'It is just that Freddie says the two of you would be very well suited,' her sister said with an innocent shrug.

'Whatever gave him that idea?' she said, wondering if there was some evidence of what they had already done together.

'He says that the air fairly crackles when the two of you are together. And, of course, the Captain can't take his eyes off you when you are around.'

'What utter rubbish,' Annie said, relieved that it was just something that her brother had made up and not anything of significance. Then she added, 'If the Captain looks at me when we are together, it is probably because he disapproves of me.'

'What could you have done to earn his disapproval?' her sister said, surprised.

There was quite a list, if she wanted to be honest, which she did not. So she settled on the answer that bothered her most. 'He thinks I am superficial, frivolous and foolish.'

'Surely not,' Hattie said, indignant. 'Once he gets to know you better, he will see the truth.'

'Well, in any case, he is not who I am thinking of,' she lied.

'Who then?'

'No one,' she said firmly.

'No one,' agreed Hattie with a sceptical nod.

Then Annie added, 'But how am I to know when I find the right man, if I like his kisses, but am infuriated by everything else about him?'

'He has kissed you?' Hattie said, her eyes growing wide.

'Do not tell Mother,' she said quickly.

'Of course not,' Hattie replied just as

quickly. 'If the family gets involved, they will have you married off before you have made up your mind.' Then she sat down again and smiled. 'So, you enjoy the kissing.'

'But everything else about the man is maddening,' she finished. 'And he insists that he does not want to marry. Not me or anyone else.'

'That is a problem,' Hattie said, considering. 'I would recommend that you be very careful around this man who is definitely not Captain Grosvenor. He may be the right one, for all we know. But if he does not want to marry, then nothing can come of it.'

'Unless he changes his mind,' she said, wondering if that was what she wanted.

'It sounds like he is not as infuriating as you originally said.' Hattie was smiling at her now, as if she had revealed something that she did not even know herself.

'I would like to know him better,' she decided. 'But he is not forthcoming about himself.'

'The truth will come out, in time,' her sister declared. 'But you say he does not want to marry. Have you pressed him on the subject?'

'Not at all. He announced it, out of the

blue,' she said, still as puzzled and annoyed as she had been when it happened.

Hattie gave her a pensive look. 'Interesting.'

'I did not find it so. In fact, I thought it was rather insulting,' she said.

'He is thinking of marriage when he is with you,' Hattie said.

'Not favourably.'

'That is better than not at all,' Hattie proclaimed and set aside her book. 'With enough time, his opinion may change. In the meantime, make no promises and allow no more liberties and we will see what we see.' Then she picked up the scissors. 'For now, I will call Claudine and we will see what we can do with this gown.'

When Will had set out for Tattersall's early on Saturday morning, he'd had no idea that the trip would land him at the Fitzroy house by evening. If it had been up to him, he'd have been anywhere else. He did not want to give Freddie the idea that he was angling after his sister, any more than he already had.

He was not angling, after all. She merely seemed to be underfoot wherever he went.

And, since he did not want to be rude, he could not help speaking to her.

He did not want to be rude, but judging by her response to him on Bond Street, he was failing at that particular goal. While it was perfectly true that he had no desire to marry, he had not meant to blurt it out as if the decision had anything to do with her. Now, he probably owed her an apology, similar to the grudging one she had given him.

But not today. He had not meant to see her at all, today. But then he had run into his cousin, George, who had helped him choose a team of carriage horses and a fine chestnut hunter. Then George had suggested a visit back to the house, where everyone was preparing to go see Felicity sing at the Fitzroy musicale, and his aunt had said something pointed about the need of family to provide moral support.

And so now here he was, perched on a bamboo chair in the Fitzroy music room, applauding politely as a stream of young ladies warbled through their solos. The importance of his role as family supporter had become clear during his cousin's piece, which was, by far, the longest and the flattest of the bunch.

He gave her an encouraging smile and sipped his lemonade, accepting a top up of brandy from George's flask as she reached the final notes. When she returned to her seat next to them, he assured her that she had done well, remarking that many of the other girls had chosen pieces that weren't as challenging as hers and commending her spirit.

And now he was listening to Lady Anne sing.

She had the voice of an angel, which came as no surprise. She had a pleasant speaking voice and some part of his brain remarked that it might be pleasant to hear her read, as well.

Tonight, she accompanied herself as she sang, which was something the other girls performing had not been able to manage. And, of course, as she did everything else, she played flawlessly. The applause she would earn at the end of the piece would be sincere, even from families like his that had come to support other girls who were showcasing their meagre talents tonight.

If the song was any indication, she spoke perfect French. The simple gown she wore was devoid of unnecessary decoration and made it plain that her form was as perfect as everything else about her.

She was so obviously ideal that it made his teeth ache to look at her. But if she was everything that an English girl should be, why wasn't she married? Surely some equally perfect and soft man had taken note of her and made an offer.

The thought made him feel even emptier, since there was no way that a woman like that would understand what he had been through. London debutantes were all too frail to take on the burden of his truth. Since Lady Anne Fitzroy was the best of the lot, she was also the most delicate, the most proper, and the most easily shattered by unpleasantness. Even if he wanted to marry, which he did not, she'd be the last one on his list.

Why was he even thinking about her in the same breath as matrimony? They had shared kisses of course, and that had been... He searched for a word to describe them. Delight was too mild, profound too serious. But whatever they had been, they had shaken something loose in him, opening his shuttered soul to the sunlight, if only for a moment.

Now her voice was soothing him, making his mind wander in directions he should not let it go. Without meaning to, he closed his eyes and drifted towards sleep, which was a thing that eluded him most nights.

And then he remembered that it did not elude. It was he who avoided it. As he lost himself, the past came back to him and with it the screams of the dying and the smell of blood and excrement and the feeling of helplessness as the bullets rained down on the little group of men around him. There was no rock, no tree, nowhere to hide, and he could hear the distant laugh of a French gunner as the bullet tore into his shoulder…

He started awake.

He was home again. But not really. He was trapped in someone else's life, just as he had been trapped on the road in Spain. The music room seemed intolerably small and airless, and Lady Anne's voice was a seductive hint of what might have been, but could never be.

He had to get out of there.

He stumbled to his feet and muttered an apology as he pushed his way down the row of listeners and fled the room.

* * *

The Captain was glaring at her.

She could allow herself only a few brief glances in his direction and she must not let it spoil her singing. She had done this piece often enough with the music master so she could play it back to front. There was no way that his disapproval would be enough to throw off her playing.

But why did one man's bad opinion matter at all? It was not as if she looked to any of the other fellows here for approval of her performance. She certainly did not steal looks at any other people while she had been playing. But, somehow, she had hoped that her song would make him smile.

Instead, it appeared that he was falling asleep. The next time she looked in his direction, his eyes were closed, but his mouth was still set in a grim, disapproving line.

Perhaps the problem was that the song was French. Did it remind him of the enemy? Or did he not understand the language and have no idea what she was singing?

But that hardly seemed likely. He must have learned something of it in school.

Maybe it was simply that he didn't like her.

Had her behaviour on the night of the bacchanal been so shocking that he thought her a fraud? For a moment, she feared that he would reveal the fact. If anyone found out where she had gone, she would assuredly be ruined.

She discarded the idea as quickly as she thought it. To do so, he would have to ruin his cousin as well and he would likely be forced to marry Annie as a result. But more important than that, it would be a dishonourable thing to do and she could not imagine that he would ever do something so despicable. He might detest her, but it would go no further than this silent disapproval.

And then, with a final sour look in her direction, he was leaving.

For the first time, she faltered in her playing, losing several notes before she found the tune again. She forced herself to smile and finish the song, gratefully receiving the applause of the audience and congratulations from her family.

A short time later, there was an intermission and she excused herself from the room and went to seek him out.

He was in the garden, on a bench by a small

pond, eyes closed and head tipped up towards the night sky. Without opening them, he spoke as she approached. 'You should not be here, Lady Anne.'

'It is my garden and I will walk in it if I please,' she said, then added, 'How did you know it was me?'

He opened his eyes now and gave her a tired look. 'Your perfume.'

'How…?' Then she remembered how close they have been in the carriage. She could still remember the smell of his cologne and the taste of his mouth. But she thought that was because of her own inexperience. She had nothing to compare him to. It surprised her to think that he might have found their kiss just as memorable.

In answer, he gave her a wry smile. Then he grew solemn. 'Why are you here, Lady Anne?'

'Have I done something to offend you?' she asked, suddenly nervous. 'You left in the middle of my song.'

'Is it really so important to you to have the attention of everyone in London?' he said, his frown returning.

Only yours.

She swallowed to keep the words from bubbling out of her. Then she said, 'Not everyone. But it still surprises me to see someone deliberately snub me in my own home.'

'Is that what you thought?' he said, raising an eyebrow. 'There are things that happen that do not involve you, you know.'

Perhaps it was a coincidence after all. But it hurt even more, since she had hoped he was paying attention to her singing and admiring her. Now, it seemed the opposite was the case. 'Then is there something I can help you with?' she said, hoping that there was a way to make things right.

Now the smile he gave her was positively feral. 'Do you ask that of all the gentlemen?'

She could feel herself going pink at what she assumed was a rude suggestion. 'I was concerned for you. Nothing more than that. But if you do not appreciate it, I retract my offer.'

He sighed and passed a hand over his eyes—suddenly he looked more tired than she could have believed possible. 'That was unfair of me. I apologise. I was brooding on the past and it has left me in a foul temper.

If you still wish to do something, you might sit with me a while until this mood passes.'

She sat down on the bench beside him, relieved to have something useful to do. Perhaps it was not totally proper, since she was with a man alone in the garden. But it was not as if they had made any effort to seclude themselves. Since anyone could wander by and see them, it was almost like being chaperoned. Or at least she wished to believe so. But by the way he was looking at her now, she felt like they were the last two people on earth.

'I am not the same as I was before my injury,' he volunteered. 'You'd have found me much more agreeable company only a few short months ago.'

'But I doubt we'd have even met under those circumstances,' she said. 'Would you have been prowling at James's club if you were a happier man?'

'Prowling,' he said with a laugh and a shake of his head. 'That is an interesting way to describe it. And the answer is, perhaps not. But if I had not been there, what would have happened to you?'

'I'd have found a way out for us,' she said, wondering if that were true.

'Fighting your way to the door?' he asked with a smile.

'If need be,' she said, chin raised.

'You, Lady Anne, are a conundrum,' he said, turning to look at her.

'Please, call me Annie,' she said. 'All my true friends do.'

'Annie,' he said, as if tasting the word and unsure of the flavour. 'Are we friends?' he asked, surprised.

'I see no reason we cannot be,' she replied. 'Now, tell me why you left during my performance. Was it something I did?'

He shook his head. 'I have been at war for a long time, Annie. Sometimes, it feels like for ever. Now that I have returned to London, my mind returns to the worst of it. And tonight's musicale?' He shrugged as if searching for a word he could not find. 'My spirit did not want to be soothed. I feel as if I do not belong here. Not any more.'

'Are you really planning to go back to battle?' she asked.

'If they will have me. But I fear they will not.' He stretched his arm out in front of him, raising it as far as shoulder height, and watching the hand tremble with weakness.

'Perhaps you need an occupation of some sort, to keep your mind busy. There is much you can do here,' she said, giving him an encouraging pat on the hand. 'Perhaps this is where the King needs you to be.'

He withdrew. 'Do not patronise me. If I wanted to be useful in England, I would have come here willingly. But to be sent home, like a disobedient child? Sometimes it is more than I can stand.'

She nodded. 'It must be hard to have no choice in your own future.'

'If I cannot do what I am best at, what am I to do? I want to finish what I have started.' He stopped talking then, as if embarrassed at his own honesty.

'You will find a way back to happiness,' she said, reaching out to touch his hand again. 'A man such as yourself will not be kept down for long.'

'Thank you.'

His hand covered hers, and she felt the warmth of it, seeping into her skin. The way he was looking at her now was quite different than the scowl that he had worn in the music room. There was a heat in it, as if there was some secret that burned in him that he needed to share.

She stared back at him and he seemed to grow closer with each moment. Or was she leaning into him?

Then she heard voices coming down the garden path and his hand withdrew. They were sitting innocently side by side when Felicity Claremont arrived, accompanied by her current suitor, the Duke of Penrith.

At the sight of them, Felicity made a point of slipping her hand possessively into the crook of the Duke's arm and offering Annie a superior smile. 'Hello, Annie,' she said and then gave a deliberate glance to her side. 'And Cousin William. What a surprise to find you here.'

'I came to the party with you,' he announced. 'It cannot be too terribly big a surprise.'

'I mean…' She glanced in Annie's direction and rolled her eyes, not bothering to finish. Then she said, with a smile too broad to be sincere, 'Annie, it seems ages since we talked.'

'Only a little while, I am sure. The day of the carriage race, wasn't it?' She was careful not to mention the incident at the club. But in all honesty, they had not really talked that night. Felicity had been too busy crying.

'I have been quite busy since then,' Felicity said, though she had not been asked.

'Really. What have you done?'

'I recently made the acquaintance of an old friend of your family.'

'How interesting,' Annie said, looking past her at the house and wishing she had never come into the garden. But then she would not have got to talk to the Captain, which had been quite informative.

'Millicent Mason,' Felicity said, interrupting her musing and pausing as if there should be some significance to the name.

'That's nice,' Annie said, forcing herself to pay attention and look at Felicity. 'I hope you relayed our good wishes.' The name was unfamiliar to her, but that did not mean much. Her mother's acquaintance was some of the widest in town.

'It has been years since she's been in London,' Felicity said with another significant pause. 'At least twenty.'

That explained why Annie did not know

her. 'I was just a baby then,' she said, relieved that she had not forgotten someone important.

'But she is back in town now,' Felicity said, as if it mattered.

'I will let my mother know,' Annie replied, staring across the garden at the house again. 'Perhaps I should speak to her now.'

She glanced down at the Captain to see if he had any intention of escorting her back to the house, but he was staring resolutely forward, ignoring both her and his cousin. It seemed she would be going alone. So she rose, offering a polite nod. 'If you will excuse me,' she said to Felicity, 'I must speak with the other guests before the music begins again.'

'Of course,' Felicity said, sounding strangely smug. 'Speak to them while you still can.'

It was an odd statement, far too final to describe a normal act of hospitality. But then, Felicity was a rather odd girl. If she meant anything of importance, it would come to light in time, but there was nothing to be done until then.

Chapter Eight

The next morning, Will felt just as confused as he had been the night before, with the addition of the devil's own head. After his conversation with Annie, he had gone home and resorted to laudanum to calm his nerves. The resulting stupor could hardly be called sleep and he had meant to spend the day with curtains drawn, avoiding sunlight and anything else.

Unfortunately, Freddie Fitzroy had different plans for him and arrived at his house first thing in the morning, ready to see the horses he'd bought on the previous day.

As they walked down to the stables, he gave Will a curious smile and asked, 'Did you have a nice talk with my sister last night?'

'What makes you think I was speaking with her?' he said quickly.

'I saw her follow you out into the garden,' he said with a grin. 'She came back alone. You were out on the veranda together at the Lanford ball as well.'

'We were only talking,' he said hurriedly.

'I am well aware of that,' he replied. 'My sister would not allow anything more, I am sure.'

'Good,' Will said, for once relieved at how obtuse Freddie was to his sister's true nature. 'Neither event was important. I have no intention of marrying, if that is what you are planning for me.'

'You might consider it. You would make an excellent couple,' Freddie said.

Will laughed. 'What could we possibly have in common?'

'You are both stubborn,' Freddie said. 'And adventurous.'

'Her?' he said, surprised. 'She is like a china doll.'

'Perhaps you are not suited, then,' Freddie replied. 'If that is what you think, you do not know her at all.'

'She and I are nothing alike,' he insisted,

trying not to be annoyed at the suggestion. 'For one thing, she is probably hunting for a title just as the other girls are.'

Freddie gave him an arch look. 'Perhaps you are thinking of your cousin, who is to make a match with a duke, if rumours are accurate. But my sister has no such plans. She has turned down several men, titled and untitled alike.'

'I did not realise that,' Will said, surprised.

'She insists that she is waiting for a love match,' Freddie added. 'And I had hoped that, since she is spending so much time with you…'

'Not that much time, surely,' he said, counting the minutes they had spent together to see if they seemed excessive. 'In any case, I mean to go back to the Peninsula as soon as I am able. There will be no need for a wife there.'

'That does not mean that you cannot have a wife in England,' Freddie pointed out. 'Leave her here until you return for good. Our mother has raised her to be able to manage a house much larger than yours. It will give you someone to write to, who will write to you in return. A reason for coming home.'

He made it all sound so simple. But it was

not simple; it was harder than Freddie would ever know. 'Not all men return from war,' he said, trying not to remember how it had been.

'Of course not,' Freddie said with a nervous laugh. 'But you are different from most men. You have survived thus far and you will survive again.'

But why had he survived? He was not immortal. It was as clear as the pain in his arm that he could be wounded. But why had he been spared when so many around him had died?

The silence between them was becoming awkward. It was his turn to speak. But he did not want to voice his thoughts, which were dark and ugly, into the bright morning sunshine. At last, he said, 'I am not going to marry. Tell your sister as much if she has any plans in that direction.'

'She... I was not speaking for her,' Freddie said hurriedly. 'If she thought that, she would have my guts for garters.'

'That is good to know,' Will said, feeling strangely worse and not better that she had expressed no interest. 'But for now, you came to see some horses, didn't you?'

'Yes,' Freddie said, relieved to be able to change the topic. 'Let us go see the horses.'

Annie came down to breakfast that morning after an uneasy night. She had dreamed that Captain Grosvenor was trying to tell her something that she had not wanted to hear. She had woken with her hands clutching the pillow around her head, covering her ears as if she had been trying to block out some real sound and not words in her own mind.

In a way it was not far from the truth. That man frequently said things she did not like and made no effort to spare her feelings when he did so. But in her dream, there had been something even more upsetting than his usual criticisms and she could not think of what it might have been.

She stared down into her chocolate at breakfast, still thinking.

'Did you have a nice night at the musicale?' her mother prompted, trying to bring her out of her funk. 'You sang as well as always and I am sure the guests enjoyed it.'

'I missed a note or two,' she admitted. 'But other than that, it went very well.'

'And I noticed that you had time to talk

with that nice Captain Grosvenor,' her mother added with a smile.

'Only to enquire after his health,' she replied. 'He was feeling out of sorts and had to leave during my performance.'

'I am sure he meant nothing by it,' her mother said.

'He said as much,' she agreed. And she was sure he might have said more, if they'd been alone for a few moments longer. Or perhaps he'd have kissed her again.

And then she remembered the nature of the interruption and announced, 'Last night, Felicity Claremont told me that an old friend of yours had returned to town. Someone you had not seen since I was a little girl.'

'How very interesting,' her mother said, sipping her tea. 'Who could it be?'

'Millicent Mason,' Annie said, buttering a muffin.

There was a clatter as her mother dropped the cup in her hand.

'Are you all right?' Annie said, casting a worried glance in her direction.

'Fine,' her mother said, but her voice seemed as if it was coming from a million miles away. 'And what else did she say?'

'Nothing,' Annie said. 'Just that I was to let you know she was back in town.'

'How very kind of her,' her mother said in the same faint voice.

'Who is this woman?' Annie asked.

'No one. No one that you need to worry about,' her mother said hurriedly. 'But if you hear anything more, tell me immediately.' Then she busied herself mopping up the spilled tea and the conversation was at an end.

This stranger certainly did not seem as unimportant as her mother claimed. But it was clear that she did not want to speak of her. Perhaps there was someone else she could ask. But other than her father, she could not think of anyone that had been in the house that long ago.

So, she finished her breakfast in silence and excused herself to make her morning calls and pay her visit to the soldiers' hospital.

As usual, she went directly to her favourite patient to see how he was faring.

'Sergeant Barnes,' she said with a smile, pulling up a stool to sit at his bedside.

'Lady Annie,' he said with a grin and doffed an imaginary hat to her.

'I am so glad to see you in good spirits,' she said.

'You are lucky to be seeing me at all,' he said. 'The surgeon says I may leave at any time and I am waiting on the Captain's word that I may finish healing in the servants' quarters at his manor house.'

'And what is your Captain's name,' she said, 'so I may know where to write you once you are settled?'

'Write me?' he said with a laugh. 'What an idea, Lady Annie. But if you do take such a notion, you may reach me care of Captain William Grosvenor.'

'Will Grosvenor,' she said, dropping her book in shock.

'That is him,' he said with a grin. 'A finer man never lived.'

'You know him from the war then,' she said, unsure whether she should pry.

'He is the reason I am here,' he said.

'In London,' she finished for him.

'And alive.' He pulled himself up in his cot and spread a hand over the sheet. 'I was one of his men, a squad of twenty, who were advancing on San Millán.' He drew two lines with his fingers on the linen in front of him to indicate a road. 'The Captain took the lead for he would never expect his men to do better than he could himself. He could march with the best of us, never tiring, never slowing. But on this particular day, his energy did us no good. We walked into the valley...' He pointed to spots on the sheet opposite the two lines he had drawn. 'The French were here and here. They fired down on us. We never had a chance.'

'You were ambushed?' she said, shocked.

'There was no hope for us,' he said with a shake of his head. 'I was the lucky one and took a ball to the knee that ruined my leg. The Captain was shot in the shoulder, but was able to drag me into a rut in the road. We lay there, face down in the mud, for hours. But the rest of the men...' He shook his head. 'Nothing left alive but the two of us and a great big dog that had wandered down out of the hills to see what was going on.'

'And how did you get away?' she asked.

'Once the firing had stopped, he hauled me back to camp, a mile at a time.'

'Even though he was wounded?' she said in awe.

'He carried me the whole way on his good

shoulder. And when they had to take my leg, he was at my bedside when I woke up and promised me a job when I was well. Then, he arranged for me to be sent here to recover,' the Sergeant said with a proud smile. 'He is the finest man who ever walked the earth.'

'He told me nothing of the attack that caused his injury,' she said softly. 'He never speaks of the war, other than his desire to return to it. And you are going to work in his stables, after you leave here?'

'I am more than happy to do so,' he said. 'I owe him my life.' He spoke with such admiration that Annie could not help a swell of excitement when she thought of the Captain. It was a shame that the man had only the most base interest in her for she wanted to know this new side of him better.

'And here is the man himself,' he said with a proud grin, snapping a salute at the approaching Captain.

'Lady Anne,' Captain Grosvenor said in a shocked voice, as if she was the last person he expected to find.

'How wonderful that you know one another,' the Sergeant said, his face almost splitting with his grin. 'This is the angel I told you about, Captain.'

'She reads to you,' the Captain said in a weak voice, staring at her in amazement.

'Novels,' she said firmly, ready to contradict him if he meant to argue for something more edifying.

'I never expected to find you here.'

'I don't know why not,' she said, annoyed as usual. 'Many of my acquaintance do something to help with the care of our brave soldiers. We knit socks, for example. And write letters.'

'Although socks are always welcome, letters for the average soldier would be quite useless. You must have noticed that few of them can read.'

'That does not mean that they do not appreciate it when others do,' she said, then added, 'And what are you doing here, Captain? It has nothing to do with your injury, I hope.'

'My arm is fine,' he said quickly. 'I am here to visit the Sergeant.'

She nodded. 'He mentioned that it was his Captain who arranged for him to be transported here, but I have only just today realised that it was you. He was just telling me of your heroism the day you were injured.'

At this, he sucked in a breath as though she had struck him rather than complimented him. His face was bloodless, as was his tone. 'There is nothing heroic about losing nineteen men, Lady Anne. It was an abject failure on my part.'

'You could not have known,' she said softly.

'I could have stayed with them,' he replied, as if this was the answer to all his problems.

'And let me die as well,' Barnes said in a sharp voice that seemed to snap him out of his mood. 'I would not have made it back to camp without you. And without your report, the next company down that road might have died as well.'

'It does not matter,' the Captain said with a laugh. 'Can't you see? None of it matters.'

'Then why do you want to go back?' she said.

'Because I do not deserve to rest when others are still in danger. And I certainly have not earned the right to my brother's inheritance. This is not who I am supposed to be.' His voice was shrill and he partnered it with a wild gesture as if to encompass everything about him, only to grimace in pain and clutch his bad shoulder. Then, before they could say anything more, he turned and walked away.

Chapter Nine

He had made a fool of himself, waving his arms and raving like a madman. And he had done it in front of the only two people whose good opinions he valued.

This last was a surprise for him. While he valued the Sergeant as the last link to his old life, his old self, he had not really thought about Annie's good opinion until he was afraid of losing it. She had stared at him just now with such confusion and disappointment that he could not bear to be near her.

Had she thought him some kind of hero? If she'd been listening to Barnes, it was quite possible. But neither of them was aware that he had been sent home from Spain for his shattered nerves as much as the damage to his arm. There was no place in battle for a

commander who shook at the sound of gun-
fire and screamed himself awake whenever
he fell asleep.

He went back to his coach and signalled
the driver to wait, then climbed into the body
and greeted the friend waiting for him there.
'Hello, Nelson.'

The big dog lumbered up from the floor
where he had been sleeping to lay his shaggy
head on his master's knee.

'I shamed myself again,' he said with a wry
smile.

The shaggy tail thumped on the floor in
happy ignorance of the truth. To Nelson, he
could do no wrong.

He stroked the dog's head and could feel
calm returning. 'She must think I'm mad,' he
said with a sigh. 'Perhaps I am. But I would
prefer that she did not know the truth.'

'Captain?' Was it his imagination, or did
he hear her voice? He offered a silent prayer
that she had not followed him out on to the
street to see after him. And, as with all of his
other prayers, it went unanswered.

'Captain Grosvenor?' She was standing on
the pavement in front of the hospital, looking
up and down the street, trying to find him.

He leaned back in his seat, out of sight of the carriage window. All he had to do was remain here in silence and she needn't find him.

But Nelson had other ideas. Perhaps he recognised his master's name, or simply had a bit of the devil in him, but he burst from the carriage and launched himself at Lady Anne as if she was his last friend in the world.

She held out a hand to ward him off, and said, 'No', in a loud, firm voice, which would have been enough to put a terrier in its place. But perhaps Nelson had forgotten the meaning of the word for he gave a woof of joy and barrelled into her, knocking her to the ground and searching her still outstretched hand for treats.

Will dived after him, too late to stop the disaster from happening, unable to do anything more than stare as she gasped for breath from her place on the ground. Her immaculate day dress was torn, her spencer stained with the mud of the street.

For a moment, she could not seem to breathe at all, her mouth still open in a shocked 'Oh'. Then, as he stood over her, trying to decide how to proceed, the wind rushed back into her in a gasp.

'Nelson, get off her,' he said, pushing the dog back and reaching down to take her by the shoulders and sit her up. 'Lady Anne, I am so sorry. Nelson is poorly trained, and it is only my fault.'

'It seems he is no better at dealing with ladies than you are,' she said. She smiled to show she had meant it as a joke, but her voice was still weak and shaky.

Then, as if to demonstrate his sorrow, Nelson pushed his face into hers and offered her a long, wet, apologetic kiss that left her cheek slimy and her bonnet askew. A moment ago, she had been a perfect confection of ruffles and bows. Now, she was destroyed.

He held his breath, waiting for the flood of tears that was sure to erupt once she realised what had happened.

Instead, she laughed. Then she threw her arms around Nelson's neck and drew him back, giving him a hug and a pat that made his tail wag even harder. 'You are a very bad dog,' she said with a grin. 'Oh, yes, you are.'

He grinned back, showing no sign that he understood her at all.

'Is he yours?' she said, allowing Will to lift her to her feet. Even with the injury to his arm, she felt as light as a feather and he had to resist the urge to hold her for longer than was needed.

He forced his arms to his sides, reminding himself that she was perfectly capable of standing on her own. 'I apologise for his greeting. I did not think he would try to get out of the carriage. I should have kept a grip on his collar.'

'It is all right,' she said. Even now that she was on her feet she had to reach up to touch the dog's head. 'Was this the dog Sergeant Barnes told me about? The one that found you on the day of—' She broke off, as though afraid to remind him of the past.

'In Spain,' he said with a shrug. 'He would not leave me alone. As I started back towards camp, he trailed along as if he was trying to help. Eventually, I gave up trying to scare him off and let him stay with me. He waited outside the tent as the surgeon removed the bullet from my shoulder and slept at the foot of my cot as I recovered.'

'You inspire loyalty in animals as well as people,' she said with a smile. 'Sergeant Barnes is quite devoted to you as well.'

'Barnes is a good fellow,' he said gruffly.

And when you came home, you had to bring him along. And the dog as well,' she said, giving Nelson another pat.

'He likes you,' he said, both surprised and annoyed.

'I like him as well,' she said, smiling. 'Who is a good doggy, then? Is it you?'

Nelson responded by plopping down beside her, tongue lolling and head butting against her hand, eager to be petted.

Then, to Will's surprise and the dog's delight, she kissed him on top of his shaggy head. He'd received nothing like this in Spain, nothing as much as the occasional extra bone at supper. But today he had the love of a beautiful woman who was not the least bit put off by his mangey appearance.

Suddenly Will felt an intense longing to lay down his troubles and sit quietly, as the dog did, letting her ease away the hurt.

The idea was ridiculous. The fact that she was petting his dog did not mean that she had the strength or patience to put up with his moods and troubles. Kindness to the Sergeant did not mean that she wanted to sit in Will's parlour on endless nights, reading novels and writing to his mother.

At the moment, she was so focused on the dog that Will wondered if she remembered him at all. It was just as well for it gave him time to ponder his next move. Should he offer to pay for the ruin of her clothing, or was it better manners to pretend that nothing had happened? She did not seem to notice for herself. She had lain on the ground as if it was the sort of collision that happened every day and she was still treating her attacker as if he was some returning hero, talking sweetly to him, as if his bad behaviour to her was some sort of virtue.

'May I offer you a ride home to change?' he said at last, making an awkward gesture towards the carriage.

'That would be most helpful,' she said, grinning at him. 'I must look a fright.'

'A bit mussed,' he said at last, then busied himself with opening the door and putting out the step, signalling the dog to get in ahead of them. Once they were all inside, the driver started towards the Fitzroy house and Lady Annie finally turned her attention back to Will.

'Now,' she said, 'what's this nonsense about

going back to war and not deserving the peace you have earned?'

The question hit him like a punch in the gut and he was left, jaw gaping, unable to answer.

'You must know that there are those who would miss you, if you rushed back to Spain, and miss you all the more if you died because you did not go with your full strength intact. What would Nelson do, for example?'

'The dog?' he said, somewhat annoyed.

'In his way, he is working to keep you alive. I am sure he would miss you terribly, as would Barnes, and your mother. I assume you have one,' she added. 'I believe I sent her a letter of condolence when Edward died.'

And what about you?

The question was too presumptuous to ask. They barely knew each other, after all. But she deserved some answer, for the question was a good one. 'I realise that my wish to go back to the war might displease others. But that does not change the way I feel. Since the day of the ambush, I have not felt like myself. The best way I can describe it is that it feels like a great error has been committed that left me here when so many other men were taken.

They had people to miss them as well and it did not matter one bit when the end came.'

Now she was giving him the worried look that so many other people had given him, when he could not manage to tell them about the glories of war and his desire for adventure. And he waited to see her expression change from one of pity to rejection.

Instead, she reached towards him, clasping his hands in hers. 'I cannot begin to understand how you manage. What can I do to help? Is there anything I can do?' She blinked at him, her bright blue eyes shining with unshed tears.

For him. She was crying in sympathy, not pity. And she wasn't frightened away.

Something in him lurched, like a cog in a machine that had been loose but had dropped back into position. He smiled and squeezed her hands, feeling her warmth streaming back into his frozen soul. 'You have done much, just by listening to me. Thank you, Lady Anne.'

'Annie,' she reminded him and rewarded him with a smile of such beauty that it stopped his breath.

They were pulling up in front of the Fitzroy house now and the groom was coming to the door to help her down. As she reached the ground, she turned back and said, 'Will I see you at Dorothea's dinner tonight?'

'I will be there,' he said, surprised to feel himself blush with eagerness at the thought of meeting her again.

'Until then,' she said. And then, she was gone, running up the drive to her door.

Chapter Ten

'Annie, what have you done?' Her mother was looking at her in horror as she rushed past the morning room, on her way to her bedroom.

'I was playing with a dog,' she admitted, staring down at her mud-covered gloves in dismay. Then she turned and looked at her reflection in the hall mirrors.

'Oh, my Lord, I look a fright.'

'I hope no one important saw you,' her mother said with a dismayed shake of her head. 'You know, for your Season, you must always look your best.'

'No one but Captain Grosvenor,' she said, staring in the mirror. 'It was his dog.'

Her mother sighed, obviously disappointed. 'You must be sure to look better tonight, so that he realises such behaviour is an aberration.'

'He did not seem to mind,' she said, hoping that was really the case. They had been having an important conversation, after all. He would not have opened his heart to her if he had been put off by her appearance.

Her mother gave her a doubtful look.

Annie sighed. 'I will do better tonight.' Then she hurried to her room to wash away the mud of the afternoon and to prepare for dinner.

That night was Freddie and Dorothea's first dinner party as a married couple and there was no way Will could refuse the invitation. Since both the Claremont and Fitzroy families would be invited, it was likely that there would be another effort to match him with Lady Anne.

Annie, he reminded himself and felt his spirit give a lurch of surprise. They had got on surprisingly well when talking today, not arguing at all. But he doubted it would go as easy tonight, since he was not suited to the sort of prolonged and polite conversation that would be expected of him at a dinner party.

It was a relief to discover that she was across the table from him rather than at his side, to the left of the Duke of Penrith and just down the table from Felicity.

Dorothea had seated him between two older, married ladies, probably aware of the fact that he was not hunting for a match. With luck, they would be garrulous enough so that he would have to do little more than nod and smile to carry his end of the conversation.

As they were seated, he offered a quick greeting to Annie, since it seemed rude not to acknowledge her at all. 'You have recovered from the incident with Nelson, I see,' he said.

'It was nothing,' she assured him.

'All the same, I am sorry for the trouble he caused you.'

'It gave us a chance to talk,' she replied.

'You enquired after my mother, as I recall. I received a letter from her today.'

'And is she well?' she asked automatically.

'She is missing Edward, of course. But she is glad that I am home,' he said with a slight frown.

'And hopes that you will remain so, I am sure,' Annie said, sampling the soup that had been set before them.

He gave a shrug in response and felt the tightness in his shoulder as he did so. Perhaps staying here would be for the best. But if he did so, what was he to do with his time? Then the rest of the first course arrived and he did his duty and spoke to the older lady at his left, asking if she was enjoying the evening.

As he had hoped, the single question resulted in a half-hour monologue on the woman's health and interests, allowing him no space other than to nod appreciatively.

When it was time to speak to the bishop's wife on his other side, she looked at him with a surprising intensity and said, 'Are you the William Grosvenor who was at the Battle of Salamanca?'

At the mention of his service, he tensed, unsure of what might be coming next. 'I was at that battle and many others.'

'Why, this is wonderful,' she said with a toothy smile. 'We saw the re-enactment of Salamanca at a theatre just this week. They had horses and sword fights, and more than a hundred actors. And you were a featured character.'

'How interesting,' he said, horrified. Good

men had died that day and he had left the field splattered with the blood of the enemy. But in London, the people viewed it as a night of entertainment. The place was more barbarous than anything he had seen in Spain.

'You must have very interesting stories to tell, after so long away.'

He could feel the blood leaving his face as the memories of the war came back to him. And next to him, a woman who he had imagined was the epitome of meekness and propriety was staring at him, hungry for his version of the truth. 'Stories? Not particularly.'

'But surely there is something you could share,' she said, nudging him in his bad arm to encourage him. 'And you really must go to the theatre, the next time you are able. I hear that there is a production of the Battle of Vitoria that has a packed house every night. Imagine it. Hundreds of men charging back and forth, duelling and dying. It is great fun.'

He reached for his wine to steady his nerves and his hand shook so hard that he spilled half of it on the tablecloth.

'I am sure your stories would be even more grand,' she said, taking a large bite of bloody beef and chewing enthusiastically.

He tried to look away. But all he could think of when he saw her attack the roast was the rumours he had heard of the French eating their own dead to avoid starving in Russia. Perhaps that was the story she wanted to hear. Or the raping and pillaging after Badajoz. The men had acted like animals then and the officers could do nothing to control them.

He could tell them the truth. But they didn't want to hear it. They wanted spectacle. They wanted glory.

Without saying another word, he threw his napkin aside and left the table.

'How rude.' The bishop's wife on the other side of the table let out an exclamation of shock as the Captain disappeared from the table, then turned to the gentleman on her other side and continued to talk.

Annie looked up with a worried frown. She had heard snatches of the conversation he'd shared with the woman beside him. Something about war stories and glorious battle. Obviously, it had pained him to a point where it was unbearable.

She continued with her meal, keeping up an uneasy conversation with the Duke at her side and watching the door for the Captain's return. But dessert came and went and the seat across the table stayed empty. Where had he got to?

When she could find a reason to excuse herself from the table, she went after him, searching first the house, then wandering out into the darkness of the garden.

'Here.' The single, soft word came from out of the shadows and she turned towards it, feeling her way around the trunk of a tree to find him behind it, leaning against the bark. She could barely see him in the gloom, but could feel the wool of his red coat and the cool lines of braid on his forearm as she grasped it.

'Are you well?' she asked, giving his arm an encouraging squeeze.

'Frankly, no,' he said, though she could hear a smile in his voice. 'Better than I was a half-hour ago. But that is not saying much.'

'That woman did not know what she was saying,' she whispered urgently to him.

Then his fist balled. 'I could not sit at table tonight and hear of the mockery they are making of the battles we have fought.'

'They mean it as honour,' she said.

'The war is not a farce to be played for the entertainment of the *ton*,' he replied.

'I know that,' she whispered, 'Because I can see what it has done to you.' At this, she could not bear his pain any longer and reached out to him, holding him in her arms and stroking the back of his neck until she felt him relax into her, as if he were dropping a burden after carrying it a long distance.

His forehead touched hers and he gave a weak laugh. 'You must think me an utter fool for behaving the way I do.'

'Not at all,' she murmured. 'The soldiers in the hospital have been quite frank about how hard it was on them and how hard it is to adjust to life at home.'

'There is no help for them, when they return,' he said with a shake of his head. 'Broken men with no futures, turned out on the streets to beg when their bodies are no longer fit service.'

'You are luckier than most, though I am sure you don't think so,' she reminded him. 'You have a house and money.'

She could feel the gentle shake of his head against hers. 'And what good does it do me?'

'Perhaps it is not meant for your good,' she

suggested. 'If you do not want it for yourself, then use it for the good of others. If you wanted to, you could help the soldiers here. You could be so much more useful than I am, with my letter writing and sock knitting.'

'You are more useful to them than you can possibly know,' he said, giving her a little shake. 'To them and to me.' Then his mouth came down on hers in a slow, sweet kiss. He tasted of wine and sorrow and she wondered if she was truly helping him, or if it was just something she wanted to believe to justify the way she behaved when she was with him. Was this what love was? This overriding need to be with him, to ease his pain and to bring him back to the man she knew he could be?

His hands were on her body now, with touches gentle as a butterfly's wing. Perhaps he did not want to muss her gown, or perhaps he was simply seeking a moment of grace and not the passion that they both craved.

But she was not afraid of him and took the opportunity to touch him in return, one hand at the back of his neck and the other pressed to his chest so she could feel the beating of his stalwart heart. It thumped steadily under her hand and her fingers pulsed against his coat in the same rhythm to remind him that, though he seemed to have doubts, it was good to be alive and here, in each other's arms.

He parted from her on a sigh, leaning his head back against the tree and pulling her close against his body, his grip relaxed but firm. Then he leaned to whisper in her ear, 'Thank you.'

'Are you better?' she asked, hoping.

'At peace,' he agreed, before setting her away from him again. 'You must return to the house before you are missed.'

'And you?' she asked, worried.

'I will follow in a few minutes so I might make apologies to my cousin. Do not worry about me. Just go.'

She did as he asked and met Dorothea in the hall, complimenting her on the fine dinner and good company and assuring her that all had gone well. Then she found her parents and left with them, without seeing the Captain again.

But though they were parted, she could not stop thinking about him. It had been a gentle kiss, more companionable than passionate. All the same, it had left her profoundly moved. He had been troubled and alone and had reached out to her in his time of need. And she had been glad to share herself with him, brief though the moment had been. Was this what love was? Because it felt different than their other kisses had been. Being in his arms had felt like coming home after a long journey.

In the darkness of the carriage on the trip home, she smiled to herself. Her parents would be happy to know that she had finally found someone she could share a lifetime with. Of course, she could not tell them as yet. He had not offered. But it was only a matter of time.

Chapter Eleven

The next night was the Claremont ball and Annie could hardly contain her excitement. She had expected it to be a deary affair, full of people she did not like, dutiful dancing and even more dutiful socialising with Felicity.

But after last night, all that had changed. It was one of the few places she could be sure that she would see Captain Grosvenor again. Even though he did not seem to like dancing or socialising, there was no way he could avoid his own family's party.

Perhaps they could be alone for a few moments again, to steal one more kiss. At the very least, she would save him the waltz. But if she wished to worm a declaration out of him, she must learn to be as serious as he was. So far, her finest gowns had done nothing to impress him. She must be sure he could see beyond them, to her spirit.

So she went to her mother with an unusual request. 'I must look my best tonight,' she said and touched her throat. 'Might I borrow some jewels? Just something small, to make me sparkle.'

'For the Captain?' her mother said, with an answering smile.

She could not think how to answer this, but her blush said enough.

'Ask my maid for the Pembroke family diamonds,' her mother said. 'By rights, they belong to your Uncle Benedict, but he will not mind if you wear them. They are simple enough for an unmarried lady and will not outshine your own beauty, if you want to attract the gaze of a certain someone.'

'Thank you,' she said and hurried to her room.

There she found her maid and began the onerous task of choosing a gown for the night's ball. And once again, nothing in her wardrobe seemed to suit her. Everything seemed too frivolous to attract the attention of the Captain. At last, she chose a gown of silver blue, that she had long considered too simple to wear to a ball, ornamented only with the diamond pendant she had borrowed from her mother. She did not bother with turbans or feathers, but wore her hair plain, with curls loose about her shoulders.

It was by far the simplest costume she had ever worn, yet she had never looked better.

When she came down the stairs to leave, her mother nodded in approval. 'You look lovely, my dear.' And then, to her surprise, her mother turned away and let out a sob.

'What is wrong?' Annie said, hurrying to her side.

'You just look like…' She took a shaky breath. 'You have grown into a beautiful young lady and we are all very proud of you.'

'Thank you,' she said, surprised and a little confused by her mother's reaction. But then the Duchess seemed to find herself again and the moment was forgotten in the bustle of the carriage ride to the ball.

Warminster House, the London home of the Claremont family, was every bit as grand as her own house, but Annie could not help but think the Fitzroys had the nicer of the two. Like everything else about the Claremonts, the place was stiff and formal and parties there never seemed as lively as they were at home. But tonight, her rather austere and elegant dress was appropriate to the setting.

And even if the company was stuffy, it wouldn't be all bad. *He* was standing at the big windows at the end of the ballroom, silhouetted in the moonlight coming in through the curtains.

She swallowed nervously, wondering if it was too soon to go to him and offer her dance card. She felt all eyes on her as she pondered and assured herself that, at least, her choice of gown had done what she'd hoped. Tonight, she wasn't just another pretty girl. She was going to be a sensation.

She smiled, hoping she could catch his eye, but he was facing away from her, staring out into the cloudy night, outlined by flashes of lightning in the distance. That was so like him, she decided. He was at an event that occupied everyone's mind, but his was elsewhere. Probably back in Spain.

She would go to him and offer a distraction. He needed to learn not to live in the past. He needed a future. She could be that, if he would let her.

But as she moved through the room towards him, something seemed off. Everyone was looking at her.

She was used to attention, of course. People often smiled and nodded when they saw her and she had gone out of her way tonight to wear the sort of gown that would draw the eyes of Will Grosvenor and every other man in the room.

But tonight, something was wrong. People looked at her, but they did not greet her. And as she passed them there was a creeping feeling on the back of her neck, as if when she turned away, people were not just looking at her, they were talking about her as well.

She turned quickly and caught Felicity Claremont raising her fan as if to hide a laugh. The little crowd around her were not just looking, they were actually staring at Annie in the sort of horrified way that one examined natural curiosities.

'She doesn't look anything like the Duke.'

'I never noticed before.'

'Now we know why.'

She turned quickly, trying to catch the source of the conversation, but the people talking moved away the moment they saw her, as if they did not want her to hear.

To hear what? What secret was there that could cause such behaviour? Her gown was daring, but not so scandalous as to put her outside of fashion. She was wearing more jewellery than usual, but she was old enough to be allowed to borrow a necklace.

Had someone discovered the trip to the gambling club? That would explain the stares, but not the conversation she had just over-heard.

'She doesn't look like her twin, either. Whoever heard of twins that looked nothing alike?'

'This explains it.'

Explained what? They were speaking of her, if they were talking of twins. She had a good mind to tell them that not all twins were identical. There was a perfectly logical reason for the differences between her and Hattie.

But when she turned to explain, the little knot of people who had been gossiping about her drew back as if she had some contagious disease.

She gave them an absent smile, trying to pretend that she had not been listening so they could pretend that they had not been talking. That was the trouble with society, she decided. So much of what passed as courtesy was nothing more than pretence.

'Not the Duchess's either? My, that is rich.'

'They have been pretending she is family all along.'

'Who does she belong to?'

'Who knows?'

Annie dropped her fan in shock.

Normally, the nearest handsome man would rush to retrieve it for her and a conversation would ensue. A moment of flirtation and the promise of a dance. But today, the fan lay on the ground until she picked it up herself.

It was all a mistake. It had to be. What reason would her parents have to lie to her about her birth? Surely if there was some dark secret in her past, they'd have given some hint of the truth. They wouldn't wait until it came out in the middle of a crowded ballroom.

Then she remembered Felicity and her mention of Millicent Mason. Had that comment been a warning?

Or had it been a threat?

She was halfway across the ballroom now

and had lost sight of the Captain while caught in the buzz of gossip surrounding her like the hum of an angry beehive. She turned back, looking for her parents, sure that they would be there to reassure her and to stop the rumours before they grew.

Instead, she saw her father looking grim but silent. Her mother's look of horror was plain for all to see. But it changed to one of pity when she met Annie's gaze. Then she looked at the ground as if there was nothing she could say or do that could express her sorrow.

Annie was frozen in place, unsure of where to go or what to do. People here tonight did not want to talk to her. They wanted to talk about her. Her parents were no protection. If the talk was to be believed, they were not even her real parents. That meant she had no one to help her. She had to go to them, to hear the truth.

Then she looked at Felicity, who fluttered her fan and smiled.

She had started the rumour. Annie was sure of it. She was the only one in the room who did not look surprised. But why? Was the favour of the *ton* so important that she would ruin another just to draw the attention on to herself? Now was not the time to confront her, not when she had the opinion of the room on her side. But if not that, what was she to do?

Run. It was the only answer. She had to get out of here, away from the chatter, at least until she could find the truth of who she was. She turned towards the door, ready to escape.

And then Captain Grosvenor was there, in her way. 'Lady Anne,' he said in a booming voice that drowned out the whispers.

'Not now, Captain,' she said, trying to push past him.

He stood firm and stiff as a wooden soldier, impervious to the gossip swirling about them. 'All in good time,' he said with a smile. 'If you have not already promised it to someone, I thought we might waltz.'

'Don't you understand it is too late for that?' she said, rolling her eyes at him. 'You don't want to be seen with me. No one does. I am a pariah.'

'You are the same woman I saw a day ago,' he said with a sardonic smile. 'A little silly, perhaps, but no different than a hundred others on the dance floor tonight.'

In other circumstances, she'd have taken

it for an insult. It never did well to be compared to other women and declared indistinguishable from them. But in this one case, she wanted to be the same as them. The same as she was a few minutes ago, a duke's daughter, Hattie's sister.

But people were staring at both of them now. She could feel their eyes on her, the whispers tickling the back of her neck like the feathers she so often wore. The feeling was intolerable. Her breathing was coming faster now, as if she had run the length of the room, and there were spots in front of her eyes. If she did not get away from here soon, she would disgrace herself by fainting, or worse. 'I have to get out of here,' she said, ready to push past him, towards the door.

'Leave it to me,' he said, signalling the nearest servant. 'Please inform the Duchess of Avondale that I am taking her daughter on a ride around the park and then home.' He glanced down at her. 'Did you bring a maid?'

'Claudine came with us as chaperon,' she said, blinking. 'She is in the ladies' retiring room.'

'Retrieve her,' he said to the footman. 'Have her meet us at the front door.'

He then escorted her to the vestibule, depositing her on an out-of-the-way bench to wait for her maid while he had his carriage brought round. Then, as the first raindrops stuck them, they rushed to the carriage and were on their way.

'Where are we going?' she asked, staring out the window.

'Does it matter?' he asked. 'We are not at the ball any more and that was what you wanted.'

'I want to go home,' she said, wondering if she was entitled to call Avondale House her true home.

'In good time,' he said, his voice calm and patient. 'You need some time to compose yourself.'

That was probably true. But at least, now that they were out of the ballroom, she didn't feel like fainting. 'I don't understand it,' she said, shaking her head as he remained silent on the other side of the carriage. 'It cannot be true. If I am not my parents' daughter, then who am I?' She stared at Claudine. 'Do you know?'

'Know what, Lady Annie?' the maid said, confused.

'Are the rumours true?' she said, panicked. 'Probably not. They could not have kept it from me for my entire life. They would have said something. What reason would they have to hide the truth?' She could feel her lip start to tremble.

'Annie!' he said, in a tone that probably roused the most frightened soldier to action. 'Do not talk rot. You are exactly who you were. I did not think you were the sort to panic at the first hint of scandal.'

'This is not a hint,' she insisted. 'If it is not true, then how do you explain the look in my mother's eyes? Either way, I am sure that the Claremonts invited us here so they could embarrass us.'

'Might I remind you, I am a member of that family,' he said in a tone that was deceptively gentle, but clear in its warning.

'I am sorry, but I cannot help the truth. Felicity was revelling in the details and seemed aware of all of them,' she said, disgusted. 'I do not know what I did to make her so jealous of me. But she is enjoying my downfall and likely had a part in it.'

'We will see about that,' he said in a dark tone that surprised her.

The rain began in earnest now, hammering at the side of the carriage and making it rock in the wind.

'I am sure to be named Society's Most Scandalous after this,' she said.

'If it is true,' he added. 'You do not know the whole story, as yet.'

'And what did you hear?' she asked. 'You were there, after all.'

He sighed as if he did not want to speak.

'Tell me,' she insisted.

'A midwife has been found who claims there were two women in labour the night that you were born, each with a single daughter. One of them died.'

'And the midwife's name was Millicent Mason,' she finished for him.

He nodded.

That meant, no matter what he wanted to believe about his family, that Felicity, at least, had known the secret for days. And her revelation of the name hadn't been intended as a kindly warning to be careful. She had meant to scare Annie out of London.

'If it is true, then I am ruined,' she said simply.

'That is nonsense,' he said with a firm

shake of his head. 'Even if the accusation is true, you are exactly the same woman you were before the claim was made.'

'Not to society.' She stared out into the rain, trying not to cry along with it. 'My parents…' She stopped, for it seemed she did not even know the names of those people and amended, 'The Duke and Duchess of Avondale will be fine, I am sure. It would take more than this to make social climbers eschew the society of a peer. But if I am a nobody, any man who was thinking of offering has just decided against it.'

'And were there any such men?' he asked. 'Do you have a particular favourite?'

How was she to answer this? If he was still so adverse to marriage that he did not consider himself as chief on the list, she was not about to suggest it now. 'That it the whole point of having a Season,' she said at last. 'But I do not know of any new offers that were forthcoming.'

'Then you do not know of any that were lost,' he said, as if it was all very simple. 'Do not make trouble for yourself over this. The revelation is recent and you cannot know what will come of it.'

Only a man who was wilfully ignorant of the workings of society would say such a thing. Annie had only to look at her maid and realise things were as bad as she suspected. Claudine could barely look her in the eye.

And it seemed that things were about to get even worse. The rain was still driving against the walls of the carriage and she could feel the horses slowing as the road grew rutted, muddy and harder to traverse, and eventually, they dragged to a stop. A moment later, the driver appeared in the doorway announcing that it would be impossible to continue to Avondale House, as the roads were flooded and impassable.

'Can we make it home?' Will said, casting a speculative glance in her direction.

'That would be easier,' the driver agreed.

'It is rather improper,' Will said, giving her another look. 'But you have your maid with you as chaperon. And it is doubtful, with the weather as it is, that your own family will make it up these roads. They will not miss you until tomorrow if they cannot make it home themselves. And we will set out at first light, if the storm has stopped.'

Annie sighed, since it seemed that nothing

tonight had gone as planned. 'You are doing the best you can,' she agreed, leaning back into the squabs, resigned. 'I thank you for your hospitality.'

'It may not be what you are used to,' he said with a wry smile. 'The house stood empty for some months and needs much work. But the bedrooms are warm and dry and there is plenty of space.'

'I am sure whatever you have will be fine,' she said, staring out into the darkness at the dark heap of stone that they were headed for. It was hard to see in the starless night, but it seemed to be an older home of good size and lights were blazing from the windows in welcome.

The carriage struggled up the rutted mud of the drive and Will hopped out, ruining his fine boots as he carried first her maid and then her over the puddles to the front step. But in the few steps it took, her simple silk gown that had been so elegant when the evening had begun was reduced to a sodden mess.

Then the door opened wide for them and a housekeeper bustled up with hot drinks and shawls, tutting over the ruined state of her master's evening clothes and assuring the ladies that all would be right now.

'Prepare two guest rooms in the east wing,' he said.

'Two,' murmured Claudine in shock.

'For this night, at least, you can sleep above stairs,' he said with a gentle smile. 'You are here to watch over your mistress and, after the harrowing time you've had, you needn't do it from a cot in the servants' quarters.'

'Thank you,' Annie said. 'For both of us. On this night, of all nights, you have been too kind.'

'Think nothing of it,' he said gruffly. But he looked at her with a strange intensity, then quickly looked away.

She shivered and glanced down at her skirts, which were clinging to her legs, leaving little to the imagination, and wrapped the shawl more tightly about herself so that he could not see the way her nipples pebbled against the wet fabric of her bodice.

He cleared his throat as if he was clearing his mind as well and said, 'I must change. And you will want to warm yourselves by the fire and get ready for bed. Rest well and do not worry. I will see you in the morning.'

Then he walked away from them, taking a candle from a holder on a nearby table and mounting the stairs to go to his room.

The housekeeper glanced after him, then found candles for them as well and led them up the stairs, turning in a different direction to lead them to a pair of well-appointed guest rooms, where servants were at work laying fires and turning back the bedding. Nightclothes had been laid out as well and, once the servants had gone, Claudine helped Annie out of her gown and pulled the pins from her hair, changing the elegant style back to a simple, thick braid. Then she spread the gown and petticoats out before the fire and buttoned her into a borrowed nightgown. It was ridiculously long, but warm and dry, which was all that really mattered.

Annie dismissed her then and climbed between the freshly changed sheets to try to rest.

But sleep would not come. She tossed for a time, reliving the ball in her mind, seeing each smirk and hearing each whispered jibe, trying to remember a single person who had seemed sympathetic to her fall from grace. It was one thing to be a public embarrassment for something one had done. Going to a party at a gambling club, for instance. If they'd heard about that, she would have known that it was all her own fault and been properly ashamed.

But to be ostracised for something that was none of her doing made no sense at all. And this was not a small infraction that could easily be forgotten. This was a major lie, twenty years in the making. If it was true, it would be the talk of the *ton* for weeks or longer.

She still had little explanation of the rumours that had circulated at the party and only a single, stricken look on her mother's face to hint at the facts.

And now she was alone with a strange man in a strange house, miles from her accusers and the family that could give her comfort. At the moment, she missed Hattie more than ever before, in a way that she'd have called a twin's bond only a few hours ago. But perhaps that love she felt for her sister was nothing more than a lifetime's familiarity.

All the same, the idea of severing it was as painful as the loss of a part of herself.

She tossed and turned, closed her eyes, then opened them again, staring into the darkness above her. The answers to her questions were hours away. What was she to do, right now, to manage the fear? She did not want to not embarrass herself further in front of Captain Grosvenor, who had been too kind in his help thus far.

Perhaps there was a library where she might find a book. Then she could pass the night quietly and sleep tomorrow, when she got home.

Did she have a home?

She shook her head again, trying to force the confusing thoughts away.

An hour later, she gave up, rose from the bed and tiptoed to the door to go in search of a book. She found the library at the end of the hall on the far side of the house. When she opened the door, she was surprised to see that the room was already lit and her host was sitting in a chair by the fire, a book in his lap and a brandy glass at his side.

'I had trouble sleeping,' she said, in response to his surprised expression.

He looked once over her body and the too-large nightdress she had been given, then focused directly on her face as he spoke, as if dismissing her state of undress. 'I am sympathetic to your troubles. I do not sleep myself.'

'Not ever?' she said, for there was something in the tone of his voice that hinted at a long-standing problem.

'Strangely enough, it was better when I was at war. Then, I marched until I was exhausted and slept knowing I had done everything possible. But at home...' He shook his head. 'At first it was the pain of my shoulder keeping me awake. But now it is the quiet and the time to think about the things I did while on the Peninsula. And when I sleep...' He shuddered.

'You are reliving events you would rather not remember,' she finished for him.

He nodded. 'If that is what sleep holds for me, I would much rather stay awake.' He took a sip of his brandy and reached out to pour a glass for her. 'Tonight, you deserve a tot of this as well. It is excellent medicine for people who want to forget.'

She took it from him, trying to be sophisticated and drink deeply. It burned her throat, making her cough. But he was right, the shock of it took her mind off her troubles and she focused, instead, on his. 'Compared to what you have been through, my problems seem very small.'

He gestured to the seat beside him on the couch and she took it, pulling her knees up and tucking her feet under her to keep back the chill.

'You navigate society like Wellington plans a battle. If anyone can survive this, you will.'

She shook her head. 'Even if the initial hubbub dies down, I am sure to be labelled Society's Most Scandalous at the end of the Season. That will start the gossips again. Even if there is a logical explanation of my parentage, my days of being the most sought-after debutante are over.'

'Is the *ton* really so fickle?' he asked, surprised.

'Before, I was the legitimate daughter of a duke and that made me everyone's favourite.' She frowned. 'Now, the man who chooses me will have to love me for myself.'

'You speak as if you considered settling for less,' he said, surprised.

'I had not planned to,' she admitted. 'But now I am not so sure of myself.'

He reached out and took her hand. 'A man who does not see your worth would have to be a very great fool. And you would be a fool for listening to such a man. Never mind who your parents might be. Do not forget who you are.'

'It is easy for you to make such judgements,' she said with a tired laugh. 'You have no intention of marrying.'

'Perhaps I do not. But I know you well enough to see that you would never be happy with a man who would care about this rumour,' he said. 'This will help you weed out the unworthy and will focus you on the men that truly suit you.'

'Or I shall remain single for the rest of my life,' she said simply. 'And do not tell me I will be better off. Perhaps that might be true for a man, but if I do not marry, I will never be more than a burden on my family.' She thought for a moment. 'And apparently, I have been that all along. If what was said is true, they are not my family, they might just be the people who took me in.'

'Do not make such assumptions until you have talked to your parents,' he said, wrapping his arms around her.

'What if I have no parents?' she said. 'What if the life I thought I had was a lie? You can have no idea what it is like to think you know yourself and your future, only to have it all ripped away from you.'

'Can I not?' he said with a bitter laugh. 'My plan was to die in the service of King and country. Instead, I watched the men in my care die while I was rendered harmless and cast aside.' He released her and held his right arm up to shoulder height, watching it shake. 'It appears I will never be strong enough to go back to where I belong and I do not know how to face the future here. Compared to the man I was, I am a useless nothing.'

'You are not useless,' she said, leaning into him. 'Not to me.' His pain was so raw that she could not help herself. She leaned in to kiss him, eager to ease the burden of the truth for both of them.

If he had any reservations about being alone with her, they were forgotten in an instant. His mouth moved on hers and his hands reached for her with none of yesterday's hesitance, fumbling with the buttons on her nightdress and pushing it aside to expose her breasts.

He parted from her long enough to look her in the eyes and then down to admire her before deliberately lowering his head to take her breast into his mouth. As his tongue toyed with the nipple, he gave a long, slow pull.

She felt the suction tighten something inside her as if he was drawing her very soul into himself. Through a haze of pleasure, she had the vague thought that she was supposed to be resisting. She had her reputation to think of.

Then she remembered that her reputation was in tatters and there might be nothing left for her but this moment and this man, and the feelings she had for him. If he would not marry her, at least she might have what was between them now.

She rose up on her knees and stroked the back of his neck, staring up at the ceiling as he moved to the other breast, teasing it as he had the first.

'You are safe with me,' he said, breathing the words on to her skin.

'I don't want to be safe,' she replied, dazed with the feeling of his mouth on her body.

'I will do nothing that gives you dishonour,' he said in a shaky voice, as his hand crept up her thigh. 'Kisses and touches are only pleasure. No one need ever know.'

His hand was on her now, his fingers playing between the folds of her body as his mouth found hers again to smother her little cry of surprise.

It was a maddening sweetness unlike anything she'd felt before, sweeping away her worries and focusing her mind on only one thing: the feeling of her body trembling under his hand. 'No one will know,' he murmured against her throat, as the speed of his strokes increased. 'Give yourself up to it, Annie. Let go.'

She gripped his shoulders, hanging on to him as though he was the only solid thing in the ocean of sensation trying to sweep her away. Then something in her seemed to break, leaving her weak and gasping, thrusting her hips against his hand.

'Please,' she whispered, begging for something more.

'I cannot,' he answered, his hand still cupping her sex.

'It is all right,' she said, knowing that it was a lie. What she wanted was wrong outside of marriage, but now she knew why women fell. If it was anything like what had just happened, she would have it, must have it tonight.

'You do not understand,' he said, shaking

his head. 'Since Spain, I have not been with a woman. I should not be with you in any case. But though I want to, I do not know if I am able.'

'Were you hurt?' she whispered, frightened.

'Not in body. In mind,' he answered. 'When I am with you, I feel hard and strong. But my strength has failed before.'

'It does not matter to me,' she said, whispering against his temple. 'I want to touch you.'

Now he was the one to gasp as she dropped her hand into his lap and fumbled for the buttons of his breeches. 'You should not.' But even as he said it, he was helping her to lower the flap.

'Let me do for you what you did for me,' she whispered. 'It feels good to be touched. You showed me that.'

'I can hardly remember,' he said with longing. Then his weak right hand guided hers to grip him, fingers circling, stroking root to tip.

She smiled, feeling a rush of power as he grew longer and harder with each stroke. 'Do you like this?' she asked, knowing he did. His expression, normally so sombre and controlled, was dazed, his mouth open as he struggled to steady his breath.

She paused for a moment and saw disappointment there, resignation and the first breath as he tried to regain control of himself. But she would not allow it. She could not let him think of the past or the future, no further ahead than the next moment.

She stripped off her nightdress and straddled his legs. 'Do what you want with me,' she whispered, then took him in her hand again. 'You promised me pleasure. Give it to me.'

'But not…' he gasped as she stroked again. 'You are under my protection. I must not…'

Must not was far better than could not. 'Do what you want,' she said, touching her own breasts with her free hand. 'Whatever you want.' Then she pressed him against her belly and continued her stroking, as he grew heavy and as wet as she was.

'I shouldn't…'

His resolve was weaking as the call of his body grew stronger. She needed to be strong as well. She pressed herself against him and caught his earlobe in her teeth, sucking hard and whispering, 'Do what you want with me. I want it, too.'

He gave a final groan and pushed her away, then, back down on the couch, hovering over her and pinning her on her back, his hands on her shoulders. Then, in one shockingly quick move, he sheathed himself in her body and lost control.

He collapsed on her after, breathing hard as if he had run a long way to come to where he was. 'Too fast,' he murmured.

'Perhaps next time it will be different,' she said, shocked at how quick it had been.

'There should be no next time,' he replied. But even as he said the words, he was thrusting gently into her and growing hard again.

Chapter Twelve

How could anything that felt this good be wrong?

Once had been a mistake that he'd had no intention of letting happen twice. But she was hot and wet and so very willing. Her arms were twining around him and he had not expected his body to answer as it had, spending on the first thrust like a green boy and hardening ready for more.

He should withdraw. He should have done so before to protect her as he'd promised. But then he should have been gentle and that was not done either. Yet she did not seem to mind. She was whispering to him, demanding more and moving under him, trying to excite him.

He had been assured by his married friends that nice women, the kind he'd meet in London ballrooms, didn't like the act. But as he'd gasped out his last and come into her the second time, she had shuddered under him in ecstasy.

He felt like a god.

Then the feeling began to fade and the regret grew. He started trying to pull away and prepare the inevitable apology and the offer which must follow what they had just done together.

As if she could sense what he was thinking, she clung to him all the tighter. 'Kiss me,' she whispered. 'Do not worry about the past or the future. Kiss me now.'

And he did. Her mouth was as welcoming as her body had been. When her lips parted from his, it was only so they could feather little kisses along his jaw, the sort that tickled and made him smile.

Then her hands came to his temples. Her fingers drew tiny circles there, with increasing pressure, settling into a rhythm that matched the beating of his heart. Her fingers were in his hair, on his neck and face, smoothing away the pain in his head, silencing the doubts and the voices.

He closed his eyes and lost himself in the feeling, drifting on a cloud of spent passion.

He woke after the deepest sleep he'd had in ages, to find that only a few hours had passed. If he wanted, he could drift back, like a leaf on the water, into another doze devoid of nightmares and the sudden, shocked wakings he was prone to, the imaginary gunshots, the dreamed cries of the dying...because none of that had happened tonight.

They were still huddled on the couch together and, though he was half dressed, she was shivering with cold and trying to snuggle beneath her abandoned nightshirt, which she'd pulled over them as a blanket.

He felt her hair tickle his neck as she roused and then settled again with a sigh, back to her own sleep, tight to his body. His bad arm was draped over her and he moved it, smothering a curse at its stiffness, then gave her a gentle shake.

It seemed a shame to wake her, for with consciousness came more problems. He had lain with a lady and she would probably be expecting an offer in the morning. But what was he to do with her if he went back to Spain?

The thought of being parted from her sent a wave of unnatural jealousy through him. She would be surrounded by men just as soft as she was, ready to take advantage of her experience and lack of protection.

But if he took her along? He imagined the women that already followed the camp, some of them whores, others from the working class, tough as leather and strong as oxen. She would fade like a flower in the heat, dying with the first bout of fever or running in shock at the brutal sights she might witness after a battle.

If he offered for her, he must stay in London to protect her. But could he stand a lifetime here, always a step out of time, unable to talk to the people around him, unable to understand them or be understood? He would hate it. But if he had any sort of honour, he would have to marry her.

She stirred then and he felt her lashes fluttering against his jaw as her eyes opened. Then her gaze travelled slowly up to meet his.

And then something changed. The satisfied half-smile she'd been wearing was replaced by one that was much brighter, the painfully polite society smile that she said used on him so many times before. When she spoke, it was to say something he had never expected to hear. 'This was a mistake. A lovely one, of course, but a mistake all the same.'

He bit back the urge to argue with her that it had been anything but. It had been beautiful and profound, one of the rare perfect nights that a man might have. 'It was unwise,' he admitted, because it was definitely that, despite the perfection of it.

'But we could not help ourselves,' she said with a sigh, as if forgiving them both.

'What do you want me to do about it?' he asked, embarrassed by how harsh it sounded. 'I will offer, if that is what you want.' The words were cold and awkward and not at all what she deserved.

At them, she laughed. He could not decide whether to be angry or relieved. Then she sobered. 'I do not know that that will be best for either of us. You have told me often enough that you do not want a wife. I will not force you into getting one.'

'Thank you,' he said, surprisingly annoyed.

'For the sake of my reputation, we must pretend that nothing has happened between us.'

'But what will you do if there is a child?'

'I will ask my maid,' she said. 'She is French. She will know what I must do.'

'I see,' he said, surprised to be hurt by how quick she was to wish away their future. But that was nonsense. He did not want a wife or a child.

And yet he wanted her. But after what had happened, she seemed further away than ever. 'If that is what you wish, then so it shall be,' he said, sitting up and letting her fall away from his body. The sudden chill in the room was more than the air, he was sure—it seemed to strike at the very heart of him. It was ridiculous. She was only saying what he knew to be true.

But he had expected her to be less sensible. He had expected tears and pleading and a woman who would make him feel as guilty as he should for losing control. Instead, she was sophisticated and understanding.

It irritated him.

But then, what had he expected? He had found her in a room full of whores, at that damned club, and even that night she had kissed him like a girl who was willing to experiment with love as one might practise a sport. Apparently, this had been just another

game for her, no matter what it had meant
to him.

He rose from the couch and did up his
breeches, then held her nightgown out to the
dying fire to warm it before offering it back to
her. 'Do you wish me to call for your maid?'

'I can manage,' she said, giving him a bru-
tally efficient smile. 'Just help me find my
way back to my room.'

So, he waited until she had dressed herself, then led her up the stairs and back to
the place she belonged before retreating to
his own room to wait out the few hours left
before dawn.

Once he was gone, Annie tried and failed
to stifle a sob. The last thing a woman wanted
to hear after a night like the one they had
shared was a grudging statement that the gentleman would offer if she expected it.

While he had slept on her shoulder, she'd
lain awake thinking of what she would say if
he asked to marry her. There had never been
any mention of love. And that, above all, was
what she had hoped for when entering this
Season. She wanted a husband like Kitty had
in George and Hattie had in Jasper, someone

who would stare at the door when she was missing from the room and light with inner gladness when she arrived.

Though Will Grosvenor had burned with something when he'd looked at her, she suspected it was more like passion than the love she'd imagined. After last night, she understood what it was to want someone that way.

And, Lord help her, she knew what it was to love. She had felt something deeper than the rush of coupling when he had rescued her from the ball tonight. He could not have been more heroic if he'd ridden into the room on a warhorse and swept her into the saddle. When she had found him, alone and wounded in his library, she had been unable to resist giving herself to him in the only way that could help.

But then he had woken and the look he'd given her was nothing like she had seen in George or Jasper. He was not a man in love. He was a man preparing, in the next breath, to sacrifice himself for the good of the woman he had dishonoured.

If she truly loved him, it was not fair to trap him in a marriage he did not want and there was no indication that his plan to go back to war had changed. He had needed her love to feel like a man again. But there was nothing to indicate that it had given him a purpose worth remaining in England for. If she could not do that for him, she had to let him go.

And nothing they had done tonight had changed anything about the problems she would face once she returned home. Then she smiled. If she was to begin a new life as a public disgrace, she could not think of a better way to start than she had tonight.

She wiped her eyes on the edge of a sheet and climbed into bed, pretending to doze until Claudine came to wake her so that they could return to Avondale House. If the maid noticed the smudge of blood on the borrowed nightdress, she said nothing about it, simply filled the wash basin with warm water and offered her mistress a flannel and towel.

Once she was clean, Annie slipped back into the gown she had worn to the ball. It was wilted, but at least it was dry. When it came time to put on the necklace, she refused, dropping it into her pocket so she could return it later. It seemed strange to wear any jewellery during the day and even stranger now that she suspected the Duchess was not her mother.

She had no right to wear such a necklace if she did not even know who she was.

Then they went downstairs and waited in the hall as Will had the carriage brought around so they could begin the journey home. He helped her and her maid up into the body of the carriage and then mounted his horse to serve as an outrider. She wondered if it was to add another level of propriety to their journey, or if he simply found it too awkward to share the space with her.

The silence in the carriage was oppressive and Annie tried not to let her nervousness show, though it grew with each step the horses took. If she was not ruined before, then she most assuredly was now.

At least, after the shock at the party, any change in her demeanour would be blamed on the revelation and not on anything she might have done when away from home.

Claudine sat across the carriage from her and she was unable to meet her eye. Surely the maid realised something had happened, but could she be trusted to keep the secret?

As if she sensed the unspoken question, the maid spoke. 'It is good that I was along last night to watch over you. Captain Grosvenor is a fine gentleman and I am sure no one would accuse him of taking advantage. But if your parents are concerned, they have but to ask me and I will tell them not to worry.'

'They might not be my parents,' Annie said in an empty voice.

Claudine must have heard some of the gossip from the other maids at the ball for she responded with a firm smile. 'Do not let yourself be swayed by what other people are speaking of until you have talked to the people who love you and heard their side of the story.'

Annie sighed. 'I do not know what they can possibly say that will change the truth. If I am not their child, then what can I do?'

'Ma chère,' her maid said with a shake of her head, 'you are young and do not understand. But sometimes, the family we make for ourselves is better than any that were given us by blood. Wait until you have talked to them. You will see.'

They arrived at the house then and, when the carriage stopped, the Captain was there to help her down. She smiled and reminded herself that his name was William. He had not given her permission to use it. But at least, in her own mind and heart she should be entitled to call him Will.

'Do you wish me to wait with you until you have spoken to your parents? Or do you wish me to speak with your father?'

He was offering again, in his own subtle way, to make this right. But as before, there was no declaration of love and no promise of anything more than a hasty marriage to save her honour.

She shook her head. 'I will be fine. They will be home soon if they are not here already. And when I speak with them...' She sighed. 'We need to speak in private so that I might learn the whole truth.'

'If you need me...' he added.

'I will write,' she said, hoping that he understood that it was an empty promise. Now that she was home, there was nothing more that he could do for her.

He gave her a dubious look, then announced, 'I will be going, then. Take care, Annie.'

Annie. The sound of her name, without the stuffiness of an honorific, was almost as good as a farewell kiss. Then he mounted his horse and led the carriage back down the drive and he was gone.

She went into the house, looking at its high ceilings and delicate plasterwork with the eyes of a visitor. She had grown up in splendour, running up and down these long, marble floored halls with Hattie, totally unaware that her destiny might have been quite different.

Then she heard the sound of horses on the drive to the house, soon followed by the jingle of harnesses and the call of the coachman to come and attend the master and mistress as they returned home. A moment later her mother rushed into the house and with a sigh of sympathy threw herself into Annie's arms.

'Oh, my dear,' she said, pressing a kiss on to Annie's cheek. 'We were so worried about you. We could not get home last night and had no idea what might have become of you. What must you have been thinking?'

'Captain Grosvenor sheltered us at his house until the storm passed,' Annie said, omitting as many glaring details about her recent arrival as she could. Then, before she could be questioned about it further, she pressed on. 'But never mind that. What was said last night at the party—was it true?'

Her mother gave her another sorrowful hug

that left no doubt what the answer to her question must be.

'Tell me the rest of it,' she said, disengaging herself from the Duchess's embrace.

'Come into the sitting room, and I will ring for tea. This is a long story and you will hear all of it.' Then she signalled the Duke and, with a solemn nod, he came as well.

When they were properly settled, the Duchess began. 'This all happened on a day when your father...' She paused, as if the word had confused the story even more. 'When the Duke was away on business. I was pregnant with Hattie and expecting her any day. And then my brother, Benedict, arrived, accompanying my oldest friend, Matilda Lockheart.'

'Uncle Benedict,' Annie said, shocked. He had always been her favourite relative. Suddenly his kindness and favouritism to her made sense.

'Matilda was in an unfortunate marriage to an unfaithful and violent man. She had been in Paris, searching for her husband, and miserably unhappy when Benedict met her. But soon, they found all the hope they needed in each other.'

'Do not blame them for what they shared,'

her father said gently. 'Some peoples' marriages are not as blessed as the one I have with your mother. And sometimes, those left behind take what joy they can get, as they find it.'

'And the two of them were truly in love,' her mother said hurriedly. 'Matilda was great with child as well and went into labour shortly after arriving. We called for the midwife and the stress of it…' She put a hand on her own belly. 'I had Hattie the same night.'

'So, we are almost the same age,' she said in wonder.

'You were born within hours of each other, close enough that you might have been twins in truth. But your mother did not survive the birthing.'

'What happened to her, after?' she said.

'We buried her at the end of the yard and planted a cherry tree on the grave. It is the one you used to play under, as a girl. And I would look out and think of you and your true mother, together without knowing…' At this, the Duchess sobbed and it was some time before she could control herself again.

Then she continued. 'Your true father was distraught and a single man in no position to care for an infant. But there I was, with a babe of my own and a husband who would understand the need to keep my brother's secret. We certainly could not give you to Matilda's husband, for there was no telling what he might do with a child who was the product of his wife's infidelity.'

'So, you kept me,' she said, her voice shaking at the enormity of the secret.

'We love you as our own,' the Duke said with a proud smile. 'You are ours in all things but birth. And you are a member of the family, you know. Benedict has been a part of your life from the first and able to watch you grow into the beautiful woman you are.'

'I suppose I should be grateful,' Annie said in response. But she did not feel grateful, she felt betrayed that they had kept the secret so well and so long that she had never suspected. Now, she was lost.

'We do not expect you to be so,' her father said, 'You have given us so much joy over the years and we never sought more than that from you. We love you still. The revelation has changed nothing.'

For them, perhaps. No one would shun a duke and duchess for their excessive charity.

But she would still feel the brunt of her parentage. Perhaps, if she was a boy, it might have been different. Acknowledged bastards of rich, titled men did quite well for themselves. But women were required to be chaste. And there was something not quite pure about an unclaimed daughter. Yesterday, she was the belle of every ball and sought after by most of the single men in London. But today…

Today, she was not even a virgin.

Then she felt the diamonds, heavy in her pocket, and dug them out, handing them to the Duchess. 'These are not mine. Take them back.'

'Oh, my dear,' she replied. 'They were yours all along. Your mother was wearing them, the night she came here. They were a gift from Benedict. They are yours, Annie. And when you wore them last night, you looked so like her…' The Duchess began to cry again and her husband rushed to her side to comfort her.

They had each other. And who did Annie have? A father who had not seen fit to raise her and a family that was not really hers. It was all too much. She looked in the mirror above the fireplace and, in it, she saw a stranger, the daughter of a woman named Matilda Lockheart.

She shook her head and ran for her room.

Chapter Thirteen

'Anne! Come out. Or let me in.' Hattie was pounding on the bedroom door, as she had intermittently for the last day and a half. 'You can't stay in there for ever, you know.'

Anne rolled into her pillow, blocking her ears with her hands, but she could still hear her sister's voice.

Or was it her sister? Hattie had been like half of her own body for her entire life. What was she to call her now?

As if she could hear her thoughts, Hattie spoke from the other side of the door. 'What people are saying means nothing to me. Mother and Father have explained and, as far as I am concerned, you are as much my sister as you ever were. You have been since the day we were born. But if that is not what you want, then accept the fact that we have been best friends for our entire lives and I will not leave you alone now that you need me.'

'Thank you,' she whispered, sitting up and wiping her eyes.

'Now open this door. I will not go away until we have talked face to face and my leg is getting tired from standing in the hall.'

Annie smiled in defeat and went to let her sister in. Though she wanted to stay holed up in her room for ever, she would never allow Hattie to overtax her bad leg while waiting to speak with her and Hattie knew it.

Annie opened the door. 'Not fair,' she said, gesturing Hattie to a seat on the bed.

Hattie limped in to take it, clearly as tired as she claimed to be. 'It worked, didn't it? You let me in and that is all that matters.'

Annie wiped the last of the tears from her eyes and stared at Hattie, unsure of what to say next. It was strange, after a lifetime of easy chatting, to be at a loss for words in front of Hattie, of all people. But now, she wondered if she had not always known that there was something keeping them apart. She had always wondered about the mystical bond that twins were supposed to have and had declared it as nonsense to anyone that asked. Though as close as people could be, she had never felt the pain of Hattie's bad leg, nor could Hattie really understand what it was like for her to discover a second set of parents.

'You are being a goose about this,' Hattie said after giving her an appraising look. 'Mother and Father still love you as much as ever and so do I.'

'That will not stop everyone else from talking,' Annie said with a frown.

'Nor will it stop you from being hurt by that talk,' Hattie agreed. 'Only you can spare yourself that pain. You must learn to ignore it.'

'If I get the chance to,' Annie replied. 'We do not know yet if I will be invited back to the parties that are left this Season. How does the mail look?'

Hattie frowned. 'Some people have rescinded their invitations to the Avondale Ball which was supposed to be the final event of the Season. And you have had no callers as yet. But it is early and the roads are still near impassable after this week's rains. There are probably a few cowards waiting to see what decision their friends make before taking a side.' She reached out and gave Annie's hand a squeeze. 'Is there someone in particular you are worried about? Captain Grosvenor has been quite attentive of late and was very kind the night of the revelation.'

'He is also the cousin of the girl who destroyed my reputation,' she said. 'It was Felicity Claremont who spread the rumours. I am sure of it.'

'I understand that you are hurt,' Hattie said as gently as possible. 'But we are linked by Freddie's marriage to the family. We must let the old grudge die.'

'We can,' Annie said with a flash of anger. 'But that does not mean they will. I have done nothing to deserve the ruin they brought down upon me.'

'But if the Captain is in any way interested in you, a marriage, especially to a Claremont, might be an excellent way to salvage this situation.'

It would save her in more way than one. But he had been clear all Season that he had no intention of marrying. She doubted that anything had really changed in the light of day and did not intend to run begging to him for more help. 'No,' she said with a sigh. 'He has never hinted that there was anything more between us than a few common interests.'

'That is a shame,' her sister said with a frown. 'I doubt, this late in the Season, that there will be other offers.'

'There is always next year,' she said, wishing fervently that the conversation could be over.

'And that is almost a year from now. I hope you are going to stop hiding in this room before then. You are worrying your family. Mother is beside herself and Father has threatened to have the servants set up the dinner table in your room if you do not come down. He said, "If she does not come to us, we shall go to her."'

The idea made Annie smile.

'There, you see?' said Hattie. 'With the help of family, you will get through this. Now, come down with me and with Mother we will plan your triumphant return to society.'

As he approached the stable at a brisk trot, Will patted his horse on the neck by way of an apology for yet another breakneck ride through the woods around his house. Since he had come back from taking Annie home, he had spent most of the time either on horseback or in the library, trying to drive thoughts of her from his mind.

Edward would have known how to handle this. He would have kept his breeches buttoned and been the honourable gentleman that Annie had needed. If not that, he would have phrased the proposal in such a way that she would have accepted him. Or perhaps he would have chosen a woman for himself who was not so stubborn as to refuse a perfectly good offer without explanation or apology.

It was clear, from their first meeting even, that she did not have enough sense to come in out of the rain, much less navigate the wolves that inhabited London society. And yet she moved freely about it, ignorant of the danger she was in.

Granted, he had better things to do with his time than trail after a pretty fool, trying to keep her out of trouble. He was used to dealing with Napoleon's army and could do so again, once he was sure that he had done the right thing by her. She could stay here, under the careful watch of Sergeant Barnes while he went back into battle…

And if he never returned? Then she would

be the prettiest widow in London. This was even worse than the current situation. He knew how men viewed widows, especially when they were beautiful and young. Widows were women with an appetite. And Annie had certainly proved that she had a taste for carnality.

He shook his head, trying to rid his mind of the vision of her body, the taste of her mouth, the feel of her moving against him. Things had been easier when he was unable and unsure, avoiding contact with women because of the embarrassing prospect of failure at that crucial moment of climax.

He had not known how lucky he was. His own appetite had returned with a vengeance and it was focused on a woman who had refused him. And why? Did she think she deserved better? She had claimed that their union was a mistake. She was right, of course. But it was an error that many people made and then erased by marriage. They did not just sample the sins of the flesh and then pretend that nothing had happened.

When he had rescued her from the debacle at his uncle's ball, she had accused the Claremont family of trying to humiliate her.

The idea was nonsense, but it might have affected her view of him. If she thought he was a representative of some conspiracy directed against her, then, of course she wanted nothing to do with him.

If that was the problem, then the solution was simple. He had but to prove that her fears were groundless by finding the culprit who had spread the rumour and she would see he and his family had nothing to do with it. The question was how to go about it?

He dismounted and walked his puffing horse the rest of the way to the stables where it was taken by the former Sergeant Barnes, to be curried and watered. Will smiled at the sight of the fellow who seemed to be doing well on his new peg, supplemented with the crutches leaning against a nearby wall. 'How goes it, Barnes?' he asked. 'Are you enjoying your new position?'

'Very much so, Captain,' he said. 'Even more so now that I have heard of the visit by Lady Annie.'

'You what?' he said, shocked.

Barnes grinned. 'You entertained the lady two nights ago, when storms left the roads in a mess.'

'And you know this because…'

'I work in the stables, Captain. And she rode in your carriage.'

'Of course,' he said in a thoughtful voice.

'In some ways, it is much like the army. The soldiers always know more than they let on to the officers. And servants always know what is going on in great houses. Will we be seeing more of Lady Annie here, Captain?'

'I hope so, Barnes.' The question was totally inappropriate and he should put the man in his place. But given their past together, he could not bring himself to do it.

There was also the fact that Barnes had answered the question he'd been asking himself just now. If he wanted to know who had spread the rumours about Annie, he should ask the servants what they knew.

Chapter Fourteen

Now that Annie had agreed to face the family again, it was decided that she should reappear in society as soon as possible. 'The longer you wait, the harder it will be,' her mother said with an encouraging smile. 'You will keep the Fitzroy name, since that is how you were raised. But you shall be Miss Anne Fitzroy now, and if anyone dares to ask, we will tell them that you are the acknowledged natural daughter of Benedict Pembroke, Earl of Ardingly. It is not quite so prestigious a connection as you had, but it is worthy none the less.'

'Uncle Benedict will not mind?' she said, worried.

'He will be overjoyed. We only took up this ruse to protect you from Matilda's husband

and he is long dead. There is nothing to fear in the truth coming out now.'

'And I am sure Benedict will be eager to take on his duties as provider of your dowry,' her father said with a nod. 'You are his only heir and I know he meant to provide for you. You are a rich woman in your own right and have no reason to fear the future.'

'Thank you,' Annie said, secretly relieved to know that her early fears of having no parent at all to claim her were unwarranted.

'Tonight's outing will be to the Duchess of Fennimoor's ball,' her mother said with an encouraging smile. 'She sent a note this afternoon to remind us of the invitation and to make it clear that she was eager to see you, Annie.'

'That was very kind of her,' Annie said, feeling even better. It was clear that some members of society had no intention of being cowed by scandal.

When dressing, she had chosen her most frivolous gown, a confection of yellow silk with a sheer overskirt dotted with silk roses. Claudine had dressed her hair with a satin turban, tall yellow plumes and more rosebuds. The combined effect was the height of fashion and announced that she had no intention of fading into the background as Felicity wished.

When they arrived at the ball, their hostess greeted Annie with a kiss to make it clear to her guests which side of the social divide she occupied, then released her into the crowd to find her own way.

'If you wish, you may sit with me in the card room,' her mother said with a worried frown. 'If there is trouble, let me know and we can leave early. You do not have to stay where you are not comfortable.'

For a moment, Annie was ready to announce that they could leave immediately. She wanted to go home and pretend that everything was the way it had been.

But it was not the same. There was no point in believing otherwise. She would not know the damage of the recent revelation until she exposed herself to the opinions of others. Perhaps it was not as bad as she thought. So, she raised her chin and opened her fan with a snap.

'Do not worry about me, Mother. I cannot run from this for ever and I will not give up before the battle has even started.' It was the sort of thing that Will might have said to her and she wondered if a little bit of his bravery might have worn off on to her.

The Duchess smiled at her in approval. 'That is the girl I raised. Try to have fun. We will stay until midnight. No longer than that.'

'I will be fine,' Annie replied, hoping it was true. Then she walked out on to the floor to seek out a dance partner.

It did not take her long to realise how much things had changed in just a few days. She could tell by the way people were looking at her that, though the Duke and Duchess of Avondale were too powerful to be snubbed, she was no longer welcome in the same way. Girls who had been her companions since school days now stared through her, as if she wasn't there.

The cut direct. She had never used it herself because she had never known anyone who deserved it. And now it was being used on her.

She smiled bravely and ignored them and chatted with those guests who were still willing to acknowledge her. But those were few and far between and as the night progressed, her dance card stayed blank.

Then she spied Felicity Claremont, who looked across the room at her, unafraid to meet her gaze with a triumphant smile.

She was the source of the scandal, Annie was sure. Tonight, she was stirring the pot, contributing to the gossip without claiming any of it as her own. But at least she was unafraid to admit that Annie was present. She needed to do so to gloat.

But Annie was not afraid of her either. There was nothing further that the girl could do to her, after all. Annie had already sunk as low as she could. So, she strolled across the room and faced her adversary. 'Good evening, Felicity.'

'And a good evening to you, Miss Fitzroy,' she said with an overly sweet smile as though the change in name was a treat to be savoured. 'I am so sorry to hear about your recent discovery.'

'Thank you for your sympathy,' she said, smiling back at Felicity as if it did not bother her at all. 'But if I might have a word with you…'

Felicity cocked her head to the side and

gave her an expectant look as if to remind her that they were speaking now.

'In private,' Annie said, trying not to grit her teeth.

'A turn around the garden?' Felicity suggested.

'That sounds delightful,' Annie lied. Then she linked her arm with the other girl's and they proceeded through the French doors as if they were the best of friends.

'It is a lovely night,' Felicity said, staring up at the moon, full on the horizon.

'For some of us more than others,' Annie said, dropping the pretence.

'You are referring to the discovery of your true identity,' Felicity said with a smile.

'You mean your revelation of my family history,' Annie said, refusing to be cowed.

Felicity replied with a nod and another smile, as if they were still speaking of the weather.

'You do not deny that you were the one who spread the rumour?' Annie said, surprised.

'It is not a rumour if it is true, Miss Fitzroy.'

'But it is a truth that stayed hidden for over twenty years,' she said, baffled.

'I know,' Felicity replied, obviously quite

proud of herself. 'I always knew that you did not look enough like your family to be a member of it. From there, it was a matter of finding the midwife,' she said with a modest blush and a flutter of her fan. 'The Duchess had bribed her to stay quiet about the whole thing. But my maid, Lily, is a niece of Millicent Mason's. When she happened to mention her aunt's previous job in the area, I sent her to question Mrs Mason.'

'I don't care how it happened,' Annie snapped, unable to control herself any longer. 'I want to know why. Why?' she said in a choked whisper. 'What have I ever done to you to deserve this?'

'It is not what you have done,' the other girl said with a furtive look around to be sure that they were not heard. 'It is what you could do. You were there that night at Montgomery James's party, you see. If I had not found a bigger scandal, you would have been the ruin of me.'

'Only if I wanted to tell such a story,' she said, amazed.

'Why would you not?' Felicity said, with a confused expression.

Because I am not like you.

The answer was obvious to Annie, just as it was impenetrable to Felicity. She could only see the truth through her own eyes. And in her world, if one had an advantage over another, they did not bother their heads with thoughts of compassion and sympathy—they used that fact to protect themselves.

'I would never have told,' Annie said, shaking her head.

'I could not be sure,' Felicity replied, looking through her.

'So you ruined me.'

'And now nothing you say about me will matter,' she said with a wan smile. 'No one will listen to someone who has lived a lie their entire lives.'

It was true. There was nothing she could say to regain her credibility.

'I would like to go back into the ballroom now,' Felicity said, glancing behind them at the house. 'My dance card is full and I do not want to miss a single thing.'

'Of course,' Annie said in a daze. What had she hoped to accomplish by this conversation? She felt no better knowing why it happened. There had been no way to avoid disaster, for, even knowing what would happen, she'd never been able to leave Felicity to her fate the night of James's party.

And if she had, she might not have met Will.

When they arrived in the ballroom again, Felicity went back to her friends and a fawning circle of male admirers, each one eager to claim their dances.

And Annie went back to being ignored. When it was clear that no one meant to approach her and ask for a dance, she went and sat down on one of the small gilt chairs at the side of the floor. There she made polite conversation with a rather homely girl who was in similar circumstances, a wallflower with no particular connections to society.

It was not something she had ever thought to be. It hurt, in an embarrassing way, for she could not think of any time she had spoken to this girl, who had probably spent many balls watching others have fun. They'd been on opposite sides of an invisible barrier of popularity.

Annie had been too busy dancing and flirting to notice the ones cast to the side. If anything, this experience would teach her to be kind to the outcasts and to find a way to include them, should fortune ever turn back in her favour.

Then a shadow fell across her dance card and when she looked up, Montgomery James was there, holding out his hand for a dance.

'Are you sure you have the right girl?' she said with a sour smile. 'There are people who you might wish to speak with, over on the other side of the room.'

'And yet I am here with you,' he said, his hand unwavering.

Since she had nothing else to do with her time, she took it and he lifted her to her feet, escorting her out on to the floor for a waltz.

He was as graceful as ever, smooth as a snake and just as untrustworthy. But who else was she to dance with? As they spun around the room, she looked past him, over his shoulder at the people standing on the sides, whispering at them. It seemed she had found a way to make the gossip about her even worse.

'We are causing quite a stir,' he said, spinning her around and making her laugh.

'The two most scandalous people in the room are dancing together,' she replied, trying to regain a little of her old fire. 'People are horrified.'

'Together, we might do anything,' he said. 'Perhaps we will be Society's Most Scandalous.'

'I suspect I have tied up that award for myself,' she said, trying not to crumble at the thought. 'People do not like someone who has been living a double life.'

'Through no fault of your own,' he reminded her.

'The blame does not seem to matter,' she said. 'It is not as if my parents are the ones paying the price for this.'

'True,' he agreed. 'But perhaps you will see the advantages of being a disappointment. You can do anything now and people will treat you no worse than they have already.'

'Anything,' she said, considering. If she was honest, she had already done more than people knew, yet she still could not summon any regret.

'You might come to my parties, where you will find the women most understanding of your condition,' he said.

'Let us be honest for a moment,' she said. 'We both know the sort of women who come to your parties.'

'Fearless,' he said.

'Because they are fallen,' she reminded him. 'No one cares for their reputation and they are not welcome in polite society.'

'And how different are they from you?' he asked.

It was a good question. What right did she have to criticise these women, when she had willingly done for pleasure what they did for money? 'Not so different as I once thought,' she admitted.

'Perhaps you should flout society, since it will not have you,' he whispered. 'If you were mine, you would not have to worry about the *ton's* opinion. You could do whatever you wanted.'

'Yours?' She laughed. 'This is not a proposal, is it?' And then she saw the wolfish expression she had seen on his face so often and her laughing ceased.

'I would call it an offer, of sorts. And nothing we need to discuss with your parents, any more than they discussed your true parentage with you.'

Her body seemed to go cold as she understood the words. But his hands on her were still warm, intimately so.

She stumbled.

He held her up, so that the trip was lost in the rhythm of the dance. 'You do not need to answer now,' he said, in the same pleasant voice he'd been using on her all Season. 'Think about it as long as you like. I will be awaiting your decision.'

Then the dance was over and he took her back to the side of the floor and her new and equally unpopular friends.

She could hardly believe what had just happened. On one hand, she wanted to laugh at the audacity of the man to speak such a way to her and in a public place.

And on another, she wondered if this might be the first time of many that she heard such an inappropriate offer. She had but to tell her father and he would put a stop to it. But it would mean a duel, which was both illegal and dangerous. And what if he lost? Perhaps it would be better to tell Freddie, but she did not want him to know, either.

She wished Will was here. Even with one weak arm, she was sure he would settle things. But if she got him involved in this, he would be obligated to offer and she to accept. It was something that neither of them wanted.

Well, something that he did not want. For

herself, she was not so sure. Being with him had been the only good thing to happen to her in days and she was tired of being sophisticated and adult and pretending that what they had done together did not matter. She knew she wanted to do what they had done again and she wanted him and not some other man.

But how could she know if she wanted to be his wife if he would not ask? She had told him not to, of course. But what was the point of an offer when she knew that it came from guilt and not love? He was far too good at doing things out of duty and not choice. She did not want to be consigned to his list of obligations, so that she might be married and forgotten as he went back to Spain and the grim future he'd planned for himself.

Then he appeared, towering over her and looking as stern as ever. When he looked at her as he was doing now, she could not help the feeling that, while he obviously wanted her, he did not like her very much.

'You are dancing with Montgomery James again, I see,' he said shaking his head in disappointment.

She tried not to flinch at the rebuke. 'Since

he was the one man not afraid to ask me, yes, I danced with him.'

'Was that all he asked you?' Will said in a gentle voice.

'What do you mean by that?' she said sharply. She was reasonably sure that no one else had heard his suggestions, but the last thing she needed was more gossip.

'I asked if he was inappropriate to you?' he said. 'Because he is the sort to prey on weakness, when he finds it.'

'I am not weak,' she snapped.

'I know that,' he said with a soft smile. 'But I was wondering if you did. Would you like to dance?'

Suddenly, she wanted nothing more than to do so. She stood up and offered her hand.

'I thought you would,' he said. 'You like to dance. You like parties and balls. You should be enjoying yourself.'

'That is what I am attempting to do,' she said, forcing a smile and taking his arm. The dance was a line dance, but it was clear that Will was not much of a dancer under any circumstances. He walked through the simple steps like a man whose only cadence was a march. But instead of annoying her, it made her smile. He was trying and he did it for her sake.

When they reached the bottom of the set and had to stand out, he surveyed the people dancing in front of them, waiting their turn. Then, without looking down at her, he asked, 'What did James say to you?'

'Nothing important,' she said. She was not sure why she lied, other than that she did not want him to be angry at her or the other man.

'I don't believe you,' he said, still smiling out at the room. 'And don't listen to him. He means to scare you into making a foolish decision.'

'Don't you mean another foolish decision?' she said, her mouth twisted in a bitter smile. 'Because you never mean to let me forget the day we met.'

'I wasn't thinking of that,' he insisted.

'I don't believe you,' she said sadly. 'You know better than anyone that I am the sort who can be persuaded to fall. You think I have no substance myself and seek it in others. That is why you are warning me now. You needn't bother, you know. I am going to refuse him.'

'But you have not done so already,' he said.

And why hadn't she? She'd had the opportunity to do it and had remained silent. It made her wonder if there wasn't something in his suspicion, after all.

'I am not going to say yes to him,' she said firmly. 'You do not have to worry about me any longer.' That meant he could go back to war with a clean conscience and leave her to whatever fate had in store for her. Which she suspected wasn't much of anything.

He smiled and nodded in approval. And then the dance began again and they had no time to talk.

Will stared out at the crowd, if only to keep his eyes off the woman next to him. If he stared at her too long, people would surely guess that he was imagining her out of the ridiculous gown she was wearing and as she had been the last night they'd been together, hair down and gloriously bare.

That woman had been much more accessible than the fashion plate she was tonight, primped and proper, as sweet and delicate as a marzipan flower. It made him wonder what he was doing here beside her, trudging through the Sir Roger de Coverley. They belonged in two different worlds.

He had meant to stay away from her to-night, for the thought of being unable to touch her was surprisingly painful. But he had seen her in the arms of James and the urge to be with her had been too much to resist. The brief hand clasps and passing smiles of this dance were nothing compared to the closeness of the waltz that she had allowed the other man.

Was she trying to drive him mad?

He did not think she was the sort of woman that took pleasure in pitting one man against another in a bid for her affections. But then, he hadn't thought she was the sort to climb into his lap and take him to heaven as she had just a couple of days ago. The revelations of her parentage had left her behaviour erratic. There was no telling what she might do, with the pressure of society wearing on her resolve and the likes of Montgomery James sniffing about, filling her head with nonsense.

The dance ended and he escorted her back to her seat and made the customary offer of a cup of punch.

'No, thank you,' she said, looking past him

to the longcase clock on the other side of the room. 'We are only staying until midnight and that is just a few minutes away.'

'Of course,' he said, giving her an awkward bow. 'I will leave you to it, then.' And he retreated, feeling like an even bigger fool than he had when she had refused him.

She left the ball a short time later, as she had said she would, and he wandered about the party for a few hours more, hiding in the smoking room and drinking far too much punch. Then it occurred to him that he had not seen James in some time either. The fellow had probably gone on to his club to game into the wee hours and practise all manner of vice.

At least he was sure that Annie was safely home and would stay out of trouble, for a little while. But men like Montgomery James were not used to taking no for an answer, or in giving up at the first refusal. He had seen something in Annie from the first, probably that bright flame of passion that Will had uncovered, the one that he didn't want other men to see.

Of course, it was up to the lady who would

share her bed in the future and she had already turned Will down. He shrugged and reminded himself that it did not matter. It was not as if he had wanted to get married and he should be relieved that he did not have to.

But that did not mean that he would let her fall into the hands of a scoundrel. He had made love to the woman. As a gentleman he felt a certain responsibility to see to her future happiness.

Perhaps it was not with him, but it certainly wasn't with Montgomery James and he would damn well see to that.

He made his excuses to the hostess and called for his carriage to take him back into London, to James's club. This time, he did not bother with the little black token and the idea that there was some special honour in being admitted to a flesh pit. He simply gave the man guarding the door a deadly stare and watched him fade into the background.

Then he worked his way through the smoky darkness to the table where James sat with a girl in his lap, raking in the pot from his latest hand of cards, oblivious to the hell that was about to rain down on him.

Will stood beside his chair, towering over him and waiting for acknowledgement.

The man looked up from his drink and pushed the girl away. Then he looked up at Will with an annoyed expression. 'Grosvenor, isn't it? What do you want with me?'

'You are harassing a certain lady of my acquaintance. I want it stopped,' he said and took a step closer to cement his position.

'You are speaking of Miss Fitzroy,' he said with a grin. 'Or do we call her a lady? For I do not know she is such.'

'She is a lady in all ways that matter,' he said. 'And in the future, you will leave her alone.'

'I think that is up to her rather than you,' the villain replied. 'I have not yet had an answer to the proposition that I put to her, but I am sure, in time, she will see my way of thinking. Then, if you wish, you can visit her here.'

Will sighed. 'I had not wanted it to come to this, for my arm aches terribly. But we must settle this somehow and I have no intention of letting you laugh away my concerns. I am not leaving until I have your assurance that you will leave the lady alone.'

'Or what?' James said with a laugh.

'Stand up, or I shall pick you up and set you on your feet,' Will said with a bored sigh.

James laughed again and pushed back his chair, standing up with his arms outspread in an open, welcoming gesture.

Then Will hit him, proving that, while his right arm might be beyond repair, his left worked just as it always had.

The man crumpled to the floor, clutching his stomach, gasping for breath.

Will looked down at him, feeling surprisingly good about the results of the punch. It probably spoke ill of him that he missed violence as a method of solving problems. But it was so much less complicated than diplomacy. 'Do we have an understanding?' he asked, trying not to smile.

'You cannot do this,' James sputtered on a gulp of air.

'Can and did. And I am perfectly capable of doing it again,' he added, wondering if he'd get the chance.

'This is an affront to my honour, sir.'

Will laughed down at him. 'Your honour? I doubt you have any of that, but tell me more.'

'I demand that you apologise immediately,'

said James, staying on the floor to avoid another blow.

'Or what?' Will said, resting his arm casually on the chair as he bent over the fallen man. 'Do you mean to challenge me to a duel? I would think twice if I were you. We will ignore the dubious idea that you have honour to defend and focus on the fact I am more than capable with any weapon you can name, even with one hand in a sling.'

At this, James was silent and sullen, and showed no sign of leaving his place on the floor, so Will grabbed a handful of collar and hoisted him back up into his chair. 'Are you willing to agree to my demands?'

'And leave Annie Fitzroy alone?' He gave a shudder. 'I want no part of the girl. Good riddance to her.'

'That is all I needed to know,' Will said with an approving nod and gave the fellow a clap on the back that almost sent him sprawling again. 'Carry on with your business. And see that you remember your promise, or I will be coming back.'

Then he turned and walked towards the door and guests and servants alike parted to let him through.

Chapter Fifteen

The next day at breakfast, Annie assured her mother that their visit to the ball had been a success and that she'd had a delightful time. It was easier to lie than to see the worried look on the Duchess's face and to make it worse by telling her that she had decided to give up. It was not as if she had to attend any more events, or to waste her time competing with Felicity Claremont, who had obviously won whatever contest she had created between them.

A short time later, Freddie arrived and disappeared into the study with the Duke, remaining there for nearly an hour before they reappeared and their father summoned the family to the library for a meeting.

'There is a problem,' her father announced.

'I am well aware of it,' Annie said, trying not to snap at him.

'Another problem,' he said, giving her a pointed look. 'Another threat to your reputation.'

She swallowed and blinked at him, doing her best to look ignorant of what was about to come. It could have been the party at the gambling den, finally coming to the surface.

'It involves Captain William Grosvenor,' her father added, giving her another look as if waiting for her to volunteer information.

Perhaps someone had seen her with the Captain and put two and two as closely together as one and one could be. If so, she was not going to admit it a moment sooner than she needed to. She continued to give her parents a blank and worried stare.

Finally, Freddie gave an exasperated huff and said, 'Will has gone to that damned club and given James a good thrashing and claimed it was about threats to your reputation.'

'Why did you not tell us that Montgomery James was bothering you last night?' her mother said, looking near to tears. 'We'd have been able to help you.'

'I did not need help to say no to him,' Annie said, just as quickly. But she hadn't said no, not really. And that was why Will had said it for her.

'Why did you even talk to James?' her mother demanded. 'You know I warned you about him.'

'Because he was the only one who would dance with me,' she admitted. 'And then, it was only to...'

'To make the sort of offer that a man like that should never have made to a decent young lady,' her father finished with a frown. 'And why did you go to the Captain with it?'

'I did not,' she insisted. 'He guessed and then...'

'He took matters into his own hands,' Freddie said, driving his fist into the opposite palm. 'He should have left it to me.'

'Or me,' her father said in a low rumble.

'Or no one,' Annie said quickly. 'The matter did not need answering by anyone but me. It certainly did not need violence.'

'But that was what happened. And now it is all over town that men are fighting over you and your reputation is suffering again,' her mother concluded.

'There is only one solution,' Freddie said, as if he had any right to dictate her future. 'You must marry Will.'

'Certainly not,' Annie said, then added, 'He does not want to be married. Not to me or anyone else.'

'He should have thought of that before taking it upon himself to defend your honour,' her father said, clearly in agreement with her brother.

'I will see to it that he changes his mind,' her brother added.

'If he does not want to marry, then what sort of husband will he make?' her mother said, clearly frustrated with the men in the room. She turned to Annie. 'And what is it you want, dear? What is it really?'

She wanted things to go back to what they had been a few days ago, when life was simpler. But she could not say that without hurting everyone in the room, so she said, 'I do not want to marry him. I will say no, if he asks.'

'What is wrong with him?' Freddie said, still eager to defend his friend.

'We do not suit,' she said quickly.

'Your sister wants to marry for love,' her

mother said. 'And, although I admit it might be easier if she were to love someone as convenient as the Captain, we cannot force her to do so. Since Parliament is adjourning, I recommend that we cancel the Avondale Ball, which was going to be poorly attended, anyway. Then we will go to the country. When we return in a year, all of this will be forgotten and we will see what the next Season brings.'

'To the country,' Annie said with a sigh. On one hand, it felt like they were running away. On the other, she loved the family home in Somerset. There would be riding and walking, and no need to pretend to be anyone other than she was. But unlike previous years, there would be no Hattie or Kitty to keep her company. Even Freddie would be in his own home with few reasons to visit.

'It is for the best,' her mother reminded her. 'And your uncle will visit. I am sure he is eager to spend more time with you.'

She meant Annie's true father. A shiver of trepidation ran through her as she thought of him. What was she to say to him, now that she knew the truth? More importantly, what would he say to her?

'Can we be gone before Society's Most Scandalous is chosen?' she said, warming to the idea.

'I think that is an excellent plan,' her mother said. 'We do not need one more reminder that things are not as they were for you. We will begin packing this afternoon and be gone before the end of the week.'

With James taken care of, there was only one more thing that Will wished to do to settle his mind about Annie. And that was to find the person who had spread the rumours and prove that his family was not to blame. He began by asking his own servants what they had heard about the matter and was directed by his housekeeper to speak to Lily Mason, a lady's maid at Warminster House.

'Felicity's lady's maid?' he said with apprehension.

'Yes, Captain. She is the niece of the midwife that supposedly delivered the Fitzroy twins.'

It was the last thing he wanted to hear and the last place he wanted to look. He had been eager to prove Annie wrong in the matter, but the crumbs of information he received were leading him directly back to Felicity.

The idea was ridiculous. The two girls were friends, or so he'd assumed. How else would they have ended up at James's club together? Perhaps Felicity had planned to play a prank on Annie and the whole thing had got out of hand.

When he arrived at Warminster House, he found his cousin sitting in the chair by the fire embroidering the hem of a handkerchief. She appeared to be the picture of English girlhood and as sweet a daughter as any family could hope to have. Not only was she pretty and talented, she was also on her way to a successful match, just as Annie was ruined.

It was a shame that the two of them were not more alike, for Annie would do well to have a dose of the other girl's modesty and quiet nature. It would not have saved her from scandal after the revelation of her birth, but perhaps she would not have experienced the pain of falling quite so far as she had from the pinnacle of society to the depths.

'You are very quiet tonight, Cousin,' Felicity said, looking up at him with clear blue eyes and an innocent expression. 'What are you thinking of that leaves you so pensive?'

'The downfall of another,' he said. 'And what a shame it is that Lady Anne should be censured for something that is no fault of hers.'

'Really, Will, you are too charitable,' she said, stabbing her needlework and taking a blood-red stitch. 'Her birth may not be her fault, but neither should she be courted by the finest gentlemen in London as if she is a legitimate child of the Duke.'

'But this sudden discovery may have ruined her chances to make a match at all,' he said gently, trying to encourage some sympathy out of the girl in front of him.

Felicity gave a shrug and stabbed her needle into the linen again. 'What I did could not be helped.'

'What you did?' he said, surprised to hear her admit it.

'Discovering the Fitzroys' secret,' she said with another demure blink. 'I suspected that there was something wrong, for the longest time. The family is simply too rackety not to have a dark side. And they are accustomed to being the most scandalous already. Surely you know that Avondale's wife was set to marry my own father, until the Duke stole her away.'

'We are not talking about the Duke,' he said firmly. 'I am interested in Lady Anne.'

'Really, Will,' she said with a sour smile. 'I thought you had better taste.'

'Not in that way,' he said sharply. 'Now tell me more about what you did.'

'I came upon the truth quite by chance. We were searching for a nursemaid for Dorothea,' Felicity said, 'and Lily, my maid, said her aunt was once a midwife for the area. And I happened to wonder about the delivery of the twins and the fact that the two of them are not more alike. So, I questioned her on the subject.' She giggled. 'It is amazing what can be discovered when one crosses a servant's palm with silver.'

'What business was it of yours?' he could not help snapping.

'It is everyone's business,' she said primly. 'Those Fitzroys are no better than they should be and Annie is the worst of the bunch.'

'And yet you went with her to James's gambling house,' he said with a gentle caution in his tone. 'Why did you trust her to take you on such an outing if you do not like her?'

'Went with her?' She laughed again. 'I went on my own, thank you very much. If there was an adventure to be had, for once, I wanted to get to it before she did.'

'You went on your own?' he said, surprised.

'It was horrid, of course, and I did not like it at all. But then she came after. She said she wanted to help me get home without being noticed.'

'She came to your rescue,' he said, trying to ignore the nagging feeling that things suddenly made more sense.

'Don't be ridiculous,' she said. 'You were the one who rescued us.'

'But she was there before me,' he said, remembering the worried expression on Annie's face as she had looked at Felicity that night and claimed to be the maid.

'And was going to scold me about my behaviour and probably tell Mother and Father what I had done. In fact, I thought it quite likely that she would be calling me Society's Most Scandalous over it. But no one will listen to a word she says now.'

'You ruined her life,' he said, amazed at her nonchalance.

'She deserved it. If I had not got her out of the way, she might have taken the Duke away from me,' she said stubbornly.

'What makes you think she had any intention of marrying your suitor?' he said, outraged at the thought.

'He speaks very highly of her,' she said with a scowl. 'And I have seen her dance with him. And she was chatting with him for half the night at Dorothea's party.'

'Because they were seated together,' Will said, shocked. 'And if he talks of her, she has likely flirted with him at one time or another. She flirts with everyone equally.' But hadn't he been jealous as well? And too stupid to act on it when he had the chance.

'And the men flirt back,' Felicity said with a bitter frown. He had been wrong to think the girls were friends. It was clear that his cousin was jealous of Annie. And from that jealousy had grown the stubborn desire to ruin for another anything she could not have for herself.

He excused himself from the room, unable to stand another moment in Felicity's presence. He walked from the house without looking back and called for his horse to gallop home.

How had he been so wrong? It had been Felicity all along. She was responsible for the incident at the gambling club, and the gossip as well. Annie had done nothing to dispute his opinions on the first and he had ignored her claims on the source of the second.

He needed to find her and apologise. He needed to make her understand that, while he might be of this family, he had no part in the attack on hers. And he needed to do something to right the wrong that had been done to defame the woman he...

He stopped, confused. What did he feel for Annie Fitzroy? He was worried about her, of course. He was aware that he wanted her, needed her and craved her body the way he craved air. But he had felt that for women before and it had always passed away. Those other women who had been so important when he was courting them were nothing but distant memories once he had lain with them.

What he felt for Annie was different than that. He had not slept since she had left him. If possible, it was even worse than it had been when he was first back from the Peninsula.

He was as guilty about how they had parted as he had been about the deaths of his men. She was like a bit of unfinished business, an unsolved problem, grown even more complicated now that he knew the truth of their meeting.

At the very least, he needed to explain to her that he did not sanction what his cousin had done to her. But words were hardly enough in this case. There had to be something he could do to make up for the wrongs that had been committed against her.

He owed her marriage.

And he needed to phrase his proposal in such a way that she could not reject it. The act called for a grand gesture or noble sacrifice of some sort, to prove that he was serious in his intent. But what was he to do? He knew nothing about romance at all and no way to speak to her but plainly.

He turned his horse towards Avondale House with a barely formed plan in place. It was rather late for callers, but he would inform the Duke of his intentions and request a private audience with Annie. Then he would not let her out of his sight until she had forgiven him and had given him permission to court her properly.

But when he arrived at the manor, the door was opened by an under-butler who informed him that the family had withdrawn to their country house in Somerset and would not return to town until the next Season. He stood on the doorstep, feeling like a fool for craning his neck to see past the fellow, unable to admit to himself the truth: he had lost his chance by waiting.

Chapter Sixteen

After another restless night, Will went to Freddie's home to ask for his help. But surprisingly it was not immediately forthcoming. His friend did not let him any further into the house than the hall.

When pressed on the need to speak to Annie's father about making an offer, Freddie replied with a shake of his head. 'She says you do not suit. I think she is none too happy with you after that mutton-headed stunt you pulled at James's club. None of us is,' he added with a frown.

'I was drunk,' Will said, hoping it sounded better than admitting the fact that he was simply a jealous idiot.

'Well, it did nothing more than renew the scandal over my sister's name,' Freddie said with a stern look. 'My father and I both suggested that we would force an offer out of you and she flatly refused. Mother says she will settle for nothing less than a love match.'

'That is very unrealistic of her,' Will insisted, feeling strangely annoyed.

'It is not up to us to tell her what she wants,' Freddie said with a shrug.

'Someone should,' Will snapped, then took a breath to steady his temper and began again. 'I am not very good at society courting. But if you will allow me to see her again, I am sure we can come to an understanding.'

Freddie frowned and considered for a moment, then answered with a sigh, 'I can arrange an invitation to the house for you. But I will not permit the two of you to be alone together without Mother and Father's permission.'

'Then how am I to talk to her?' he said, frustrated.

'As other men do, I suspect. You can speak to her while properly chaperoned, if she allows you to. If she does not, the family will not permit you to pester her on a matter that she has already decided. And if you cannot follow the simple rules set for you, I will put you bodily out of the house. Do you agree?'

Will resisted the temptation to tell Freddie that it would take more than him to put him out of somewhere he wished to be and managed a meek nod and an, 'Agreed.'

'Very well then. I will discuss the matter with my father. If you hear nothing to the contrary, arrive at the house in a week and come prepared for hunting, fishing, or both, for that is the excuse I mean to give for your presence. The rest is up to you.'

Annie had forgotten how lonely the country could be.

Actually, it had never actually been lonely, for there was always Hattie to keep her company and sometimes Kitty as well. Among them, they had complained about the lack of balls and parties and had managed to get up to all kinds of mischief to make up for the dearth of entertainment.

Now that she was a grown woman, and perhaps a spinster, she was allowed nothing more mischievous than darning socks. She supposed it was better than being shunned by society, but there were only so many invigorating walks one could take before one began to think that public disgrace hadn't been all bad. At least there had been people in it.

But perhaps that was about to change. They had been in Somerset for only a week and she had been reading a novel in the garden, when she spied an unfamiliar carriage on the drive and hurried into the house to find her Uncle Benedict waiting in the sitting room for her to return.

Her father.

She felt another rush of strange emotions— anger, confusion and love wound into a tangled ball that seemed to wedge in her throat, making it impossible to speak. Her first impulse was to run for her room again, as she had after her parents first told her the truth. Instead, she froze in the doorway of the sitting room, silent, waiting for him to acknowledge her presence.

Then he looked up and saw her, and his expression was so desperate with longing that she knew she could not leave until he had said whatever it was that he'd come to say.

She ran her hands down her skirts to wipe the dampness from her palms and stepped into the room to greet him with a curtsy.

'Annie,' he said. The single word held all the emotion she felt and others besides. For a moment, his arms rose as if ready to offer a hug. Then they dropped to his sides again and he reached into his pocket and produced a bag of boiled sweets, as he often had when he had visited her as a girl. He held them out to her. 'I know this is not enough to change how you probably feel about me, but I doubt it will hurt.'

She picked a ginger drop and popped it into her mouth with a shrug. 'There is never a bad time for a ginger sweet,' she said with a nervous smile.

'You must know why I am here,' he said, as if he did not want to speak about it any more than she did.

'Because I have learned the truth,' she said. 'Everyone has. And now you can't hide the fact that I am your daughter.' She paused to suck on the sweet to take the bitterness from her mouth. 'Really, you needn't have bothered. I don't need to hear anything more on the subject.'

'Not even to hear about your real mother?' he said with a sad smile, taking one of the sweets for himself.

'She died,' Annie said, still not sure why the news gave her pain. 'How can I miss a person whom I never met?'

'You miss the times you might have had, had she lived,' he said simply. 'Eleanor loved you as her own, I know. But you have had the good fortune to have two mothers, one of whom loved you more than life itself.'

'The choice was not made by her,' Annie said.

'But she made the choice to have you,' he reminded her. 'When we discovered that she was with child, Matilda and I talked about the future. If she kept you, she would have to hide you from her husband, for he would never have allowed either of you to live had he discovered she carried a child that was not his.'

'What would you have done with me had she survived?' she said, suddenly interested.

'We planned to live in Scotland, in my hunting lodge,' he said. 'The rules of marriage are not so strict there and no one would question that we wed without a licence.'

'Life would have been very different,' she admitted.

'Simpler. You would have been educated, of course. And introduced to the local gentry.

But there would have been no London Seasons and no visits to the city at all. We would have been in hiding until her husband died, which he did not do until just three years ago.'

'I would not have minded,' she said hurriedly.

'Because you would not have known any better,' he reminded her.

'Why do people treat me as if I could not live without the glamour of the Season?' she said, a little frustrated. 'I am deeper than that.'

'I know you are,' he agreed. 'I have watched you closely, all this time. And though I did not want to hurt Hattie, you were always my favourite. Now you know why.'

She could not think of what to do or say, other than to nod.

'And although you would not have minded a diminished life because of your parents' choices, I would have cared, as would your mother. We both spoke of wanting the best for you and my sister could give you more than I ever could.' He took her hand and gave it a fatherly squeeze. 'When Matilda died, I was beside myself with grief. I had no idea how to care for a child, especially not a little girl. I'd have left you in the care of nurses.

And, with no wife, you'd have been raised as my bastard. I wanted so much more for you than the truth could give.' He reached out and took her other hand. 'And still I have regrets. Not for your birth, of course. You have grown into a woman as beautiful as your mother, as lovely and loving and intelligent as I could have hoped. My only regret is that I could have no claim in making you into what you are today.'

'That is not true,' she said with a small smile. 'You were always my favourite uncle and I wanted to make you proud of me. And now, you will be a father to me.' She thought for a moment. 'A second father, if that is all right.'

'It is more than I ever expected,' he said with a smile. 'And you needn't worry about the future, as far as I can manage it. Society may turn its back on you this year. But next year, you will be known as my only heir and a rich young lady in your own right. Money will do much to smooth over objections of most young men.'

'I do not want to seem ungrateful,' she said, 'but I do not want to be married to a man who will be so easily swayed by a fat dowry.'

He laughed. 'You are more like your mother than you realise. She was forced to marry the man she did and swore that her child would be raised to value love above all.'

'You think she would be proud of me?' she said, wondering why she cared about a woman she had not even known about until a few days ago.

'Very much so,' her uncle assured her. 'As am I,' he added. 'As am I. Now come, let us find your parents and see what plans they have to entertain us.' He gave a theatrical yawn. 'I am sure the country will be terribly boring to you, after the joys of London, but I look forward to a rest.'

'I have had quite enough of London,' she said with a shudder.

'Hello?' There was a call from the front hall and she looked out of the sitting room door to see Freddie and Dorothea followed by a trail of footmen carrying enough luggage to last them several weeks.

'What are you doing here?' she said, staring at the caravan in confusion.

'That is no way to greet us when we have come to visit with you, little Sister,' Freddie said with a laugh.

'I welcome the company,' she said, 'as I am sure our parents will. But I assumed that you would want to spend more time with your wife. You are newly married, after all.'

'It was partly my idea to come,' Dorothea assured her. 'At times like this, it is important for families to stick together.'

Annie smiled. It was probably Dorothea's way of declaring allegiance to her new family and rejecting the Claremonts and their treachery.

'And I will admit, the hunting is better here than at our estate,' Freddie said with a grin.

'Very well then,' she said with a shake of her head. 'You are here to hunt and your dear wife will keep company with me while you are out of the house. I cannot think of a better way to spend the time.'

But the next day, she wondered at her brother's motivation in coming. He and Dorothea did not appear for breakfast and when they arrived at luncheon, it was to exchange secretive glances that hinted at how they had spent the missing time. Then, instead of calling for the servants to clean and load his guns, Freddie gave his wife a calf-eyed look and offered to show her about the property. He made no mention of including Annie in the tour and she suspected that she would not be welcome should she try to follow them.

She swallowed her hurt and wished them well, trying not to think of the activity she was sure they meant to engage in. She was not supposed to know about what went on between married people, much less wish that she could do it again.

She was lonely, that was all. She was missing Will. She had to remind herself repeatedly that there was no reason to. The thing that had happened between them was her fault as much as his. But it had occurred when she was at her lowest and not thinking clearly. It had given him the idea that he had the right to meddle in things that were none of his business and he had damaged what was left of her tattered reputation by picking a fight.

If they saw each other again, things would likely get even worse. She was fortunate that her courses had come and gone since their night together, proving that there was no reason to renew contact with him. She certainly could not afford the risk of more clandestine meetings.

Yet she could not stop thinking about him.

And the way the family took care not to mention him made her all the more sure that they knew how she felt about him. Her mother had asked her if there was anyone she favoured in the last Season, someone she might wish to say goodbye to before she left town. When she had assured her that there was no one, her mother had looked at her doubtfully and reiterated that, if there was any reason at all to stay in London, she had but to speak and they would change plans immediately.

It was as if the family saw something that she did not. It was very annoying.

And today, it was apparent that she would receive none of the promised companionship from Dorothea and would be on her own, just as she was before. Since she was already tired of the book she had started, she decided to spend the afternoon in the garden, pulling weeds. Her help probably maddened the gardeners who would just as soon have handled the matter themselves. But she had begged them for a small plot of her own, since she loved the rich smell of the earth and the feel of it between her fingers.

Today, the air was fresh from a heavy rain

the night before, and sheep had been released on the grounds to trim the grass around the hedges. But when she went to tend her plot, she found a troublesome ewe had chosen to root up her flowers instead of doing its job.

'Shoo,' she said, raising the skirt of her plain cotton gown and flapping ineffectually at the offending sheep. 'You are here to eat the yard, not my daisies. Shoo.'

The ewe gave her a speculative look and pulled up another blossom, munching thoughtfully.

'Move,' she said, stepping into the muddy bed to try to push the sheep out the other side. The wet earth sucked at her boots, dragging them half off her feet. As she tried to free one foot, the other sank even deeper and she stumbled against the sheep and into the mud.

And then, behind her, she heard the sound of hoofbeats coming up the drive. She managed to pull herself up to her knees and wipe the mud from her face in time to see Will Grosvenor arrive, immaculate in a brown wool suit, sitting on a horse as though he was parading before the King.

'Lady Anne,' he said with a tip of his hat.

'Captain Grosvenor,' she replied breathlessly, staggering to her feet, only to collapse backwards, landing on her bottom with a splat.

Did she see a trace of a smile as he passed, or was it her imagination? He rode on as if nothing unusual had just happened until he reached the house. Then, he offered his reins to the footman and went inside.

As soon as he had gone, she crawled out of the flowerbed, bracing herself against the sheep, which promptly dumped her back into the dirt. On her second attempt, she made it to the grass and raced in her stocking feet to the back of the house so she might get upstairs to change without being seen from the receiving rooms.

He was here.

When she got to her room, she called for Claudine and a fresh wash basin. But once she was clean, what was she to do? She had thought that getting away from London would solve at least one problem. She would not have to see the Captain again. And yet, here he was.

What was she to say now that he was near her again? When she had seen him coming up the drive she had wanted to stand and stare.

She was hungry for the sight of him though it had only been two weeks since they had last seen each other. What had he done in that time? Had he made any progress in getting back his command?

And then she reminded herself that he was part of the reason she was hiding in the country and that she did not care what was happening in his life since it was not likely to pertain to her.

She forced herself to calm down. If she rushed down to see him, he would think that she had been brooding on the loss of him. Better to leave him waiting and treat his arrival as unimportant.

Once dressed, she spent a full ten minutes trying to pretend that his presence in the house did not matter. But she could not stop her mind from racing. What was he doing here? She had not summoned him. The last she knew, he was not even planning to stay in England, much less come to this part of the country. Had he been missing her as much as she missed him?

That was doubtful. Though Captain William Grosvenor was a man of passion, he was not the sort to be overcome with softer emotions. He might miss the war and pine over a lack of action, but he would not have wasted a minute's thought over the loss of her.

But now that he was here, she could not exactly avoid him and the longer she took to face him, the harder it would be. So she forced herself to walk slowly down the main stairs and then to the receiving room where the family was assembled to greet the new visitor. As she entered, they looked up as one, giving her the impression that she had been the topic of conversation all along.

Then she looked at Will, trying to ignore the sizzling along her nerves at the sight of him.

'Annie,' her mother said, in an overly bright tone. 'Look who has come to visit.'

'I was there when he arrived,' she said with a dismissive wave of her hand. 'At the moment, I wish to speak to the family.' She gave Will a pointed look and added, 'Alone.'

'It has been a long journey,' Will supplied. 'If someone could show me to my room, I wouldn't mind a rest before dinner.'

'Of course,' her mother said, summoning a footman and directing him to show Will to a guest room. When he had left the room, she turned on Annie and announced, 'That was very rude.'

'Not as rude as surprising me with a visit from the Captain,' she said, glaring at her brother. 'I should have known something was up when you suddenly developed an interest in hunting.'

'I tried to tell him you were not ready,' Dorothea said with a frown in her husband's direction. 'But he insisted.'

'This doesn't have to have anything to do with you,' Freddie said with a dismissive shake of his head. 'I invited him for shooting and sport. The man needs to get out of London and clear his head. The war was not kind to him.'

'I am aware of that,' Annie said with exasperation. 'But he has an estate of his own to retire to. He does not need to come all the way to Somerset.'

'Might I remind you that the family is gathering for your sake,' her mother said in a prim voice. 'Whatever the situation appears to be, Freddie has come for you. And if he wants to bring a friend to visit, it is well within his right.'

'But why him, of all people?' she said, staring at her brother.

'Because he requested another chance to talk to you. He wishes to apologise to you for the trouble he and his family have caused,' Freddie said at last. 'He was distraught. I took pity on him. I told him that it was not likely to make a difference. And you do not have to talk to him if you do not want to.'

The Duchess gave a huff of disagreement. 'What utter nonsense. I have no intention of letting you snub a guest in this house. You will associate with him as you would any other gentleman, with a chaperon present at all times. He is welcome to stay here, but that does not mean we expect you to marry him.'

'Marriage?' she said on a gasp. 'Who said anything about that?'

'Well, he is an eligible man,' her mother said thoughtfully. 'It does not pay to reject him out of hand as you seem to have.'

'I do not have to reject him,' she said, shocked. 'He has told me that he does not want to marry me or anyone else.'

'So you have discussed the matter,' her mother said, obviously interested.

'We have. And he makes no bones about

the fact that he does not want a wife,' she said. 'It is nothing personal against me.'

'That is excellent news,' her mother said. 'That means he might change his mind once he gets to know you.'

'He knows me well enough to have formed an opinion,' she said. Better than anyone knew.

'He knows you well enough to rush to your defence when you are threatened by a rake,' her mother said. 'If he did not want to offer, it was very forward of him.'

'He has a strong sense of justice,' Annie said with a shrug.

'It sounds as if you have forgiven him already,' her mother said. 'Now forgive your brother as well and we will all go to our rooms to prepare for dinner.'

Since it appeared that there was nothing else for it, she did as her mother asked and went to her room, trying not to think about Will sleeping just down the hall from her. When it grew time to dress, she sorted through the gowns in the wardrobe, searching for something he had not seen before, something that would dazzle him.

Then she realised that there was no point

in bothering for he had not been the least bit impressed by anything she had worn so far. If it was too late to make a difference, she might as well be comfortable. She chose a blue muslin that she'd have worn in any case and had Claudine dress her hair simply, tying the curls back with a ribbon.

Then, she went down to dinner, stopping on the stairs to compose herself. But as she did so, she saw Will waiting for her at the foot. Instead of his usual brilliant red coat, he had chosen a black one more suitable to life in the country. But even without the uniform, his military posture remained, as did the stiffness in his arm.

'May I escort you in to dinner?' he said, holding out his arm to her.

'At home, such formalities are not necessary,' she said, sweeping past him and walking alone.

He hurried to catch up to her, but did not try to take her arm again. 'Then I will follow you, since I do not know the way to the dining room.'

'Suit yourself,' she said, leading.

When they arrived at the table, her parents had taken their usual places, Freddie had given the seat next to him to his wife, Benedict was at the foot and the only place empty for Will was the seat at her side that would normally have been occupied by Hattie.

He took it without a word and she did her best to ignore the barely hidden smiles on the family to see the two of them together.

Strangely enough, the Captain did not seem to be annoyed by this obvious matchmaking. He ate in silence, as if it was the most natural thing in the world.

'I notice you are not wearing your uniform, Captain,' her mother said, smiling down the table at him.

'That is because I resigned my commission,' he said, not looking up from his plate. 'I am just plain old Mr Grosvenor now.'

The news caught Annie in the middle of a sip of wine and she inhaled half of it, coughing and weeping for several minutes as she tried to catch her breath. When at last she could speak, she looked at him in surprise. 'You are not going back to Spain?'

'The war will not wait for me to heal and I cannot risk endangering others due to my own weakness,' he said with a shrug. 'Nor do I see myself behind a desk at the Horse Guards.'

'It must be quite a change for you,' her mother said with a sympathetic nod.

'I joined the army as soon as I left school,' he replied. 'I know no other life. But I have sufficient funds to maintain my household and can live contentedly.'

'Ha,' Annie said, unable to help herself.

Her mother gave a warning glare at her bad manners, but Will only smiled in response.

'Miss Anne is correct,' he said with a nod. 'Contentedness is probably an exaggeration on my part. The truth is, I do not see myself as a gentleman of leisure and am searching for ways to occupy my time now that I do not have the army.'

'Dancing master,' she said, unable to resist goading him.

'Or a diplomat,' he replied and took a spoonful of soup.

'I am sure you will find something,' Freddie said, then the conversation turned to hunting and the amount of time that could be spent in the forest tomorrow.

It must have continued, even after the meal, for when the ladies withdrew from the table, the men lingered over their port and did not follow them until it was nearly time for bed.

When she wondered at it, her mother announced that Benedict and the Duke likely had many questions for the Captain, and it probably took some time.

Her heart sank. No matter how many times her mother had said she did not have to marry the man, it was clear that that was what her family wanted her to do.

And apparently Will had decided he wanted the same. Giving up his commission was a sure sign of that. But how would her heart survive a marriage to a man who did not love her?

Chapter Seventeen

His plan was working. Annie's two fathers and brother had spent the evening grilling him on his finances, his prospects and his general worthiness to be a husband to their girl. As usual, he had been cool under fire and eased their mind about his current lack of direction. He had told them of his tentative plans for the future, though he had done nothing as yet to make things official. Before he did that, he wanted to win Annie's hand.

The lady's willingness to marry him was a matter of concern to everyone in the room, himself included. Apparently, she was adamant on the subject and they were in agreement that no family pressure would be applied to change her mind.

He had assured them that he could be persuasive enough on his own to get her to a yes. But he was still not sure if that was the truth. What they had done already should have been enough to seal the deal between them. Instead, it seemed to have made her more convinced that they could not be together.

It was enough to make a doubtful man question his abilities. But there had been nothing about her response that night to make him believe that she did not have a taste for what they had done. She had been enthusiastic to the point of insistence, nor did she push him away immediately after.

Between his worries on the matter and his usual insomnia he was in no mood to spend the day tramping through the woods after a rabbit and was relieved to come down to breakfast and find that it was raining and that there would be no hunting. Instead, Freddie had stacked fencing gear in the front hall. But to his surprise, he was greeted not by his friend, but Annie.

She was standing over the stack of foils and sabres with an ecstatic light in her eyes, touching the blades with a gentle finger. 'Oh,' she said in a sigh that was close to orgasmic. 'Swords.'

He looked at her, shocked. 'And what would you have to do with those?'

She started at the sound of his voice and said, 'I am not supposed to speak to you without a chaperon present.'

'We are in the front hall and there are footman less than ten feet away,' he replied. 'You are also standing next to a pile of weapons, although I have no idea why. I think your honour is safe enough.'

She turned to him with a smile. Then she reached out her slender white hand and stroked a hilt in a manner that immediately turned his mind to places that it must not go. 'I have some experience with handling a foil.'

'What use does a woman have for such a thing?' he said with a laugh.

'I have a very indulgent brother,' she said with a grin. 'Or at least, I had. Now that he is married, he seems to think he can interfere in my life as if he is a father to me.' She grimaced. 'And I already have an extra one of those.'

'How are you adjusting to that fact?' he asked.

'As well as can be expected. It helps that it is just Uncle Benedict and not someone else. I loved him already.' Then she gave him a direct look. 'He has promised to make me rich enough so I don't have to marry at all, if I do not wish to.'

'I see,' Will replied.

'But he is not here right now and neither is Freddie,' she said, picking up a foil and lunging to the side.

'Put that down,' he said sharply.

She ignored him and cut the air with the blade. 'You could always fence with me while we wait for him.'

'I do not think that is wise,' he said, shaking his head.

'On the contrary, it is a brilliant idea,' she said. 'It is about time I learned to protect my own honour so some people stop taking it upon themselves to step in where they are not welcome.'

'I apologise for taking the liberty in your name,' he said, doing his best to look contrite.

'Apology accepted, on one condition.' She gave a half-hearted thrust in his direction and lunged before returning to her starting position.

'You think you can manage to defend yourself against me?' he said, unable to keep the doubt out of his voice.

'I know how to box as well,' she said with a proud smile. 'Freddie said, knowing men as he did, we girls should all know how to throw a punch, since it might be necessary on some occasion.'

He shuddered and tried not to think of the night in the carriage. 'I don't believe you,' he said. He had not remembered her as being anything other than willing. If she had known how to hit him, why she had not simply answered his suggestion in the manner it deserved?

'Pick up one of these swords and you shall see,' she said, her chin raised in a most attractive display of stubbornness.

He laughed. 'You know I do not view these things as the toys you seem to think them. I have defended my life, not just my honour.'

'You are also injured,' she reminded him. 'Under those conditions, it is probably unfair of me to take advantage of you.'

'It is fortunate for me that I fence almost as well with my left hand as my right,' he said, refusing to back down. Perhaps it would make him laugh to see her attempt something so ob- viously inappropriate. Or perhaps he would simply put her in her place and go on with his morning. 'All right. But put on a coat and mask. I do not want to risk hurting you.' He picked up his weapon and when he turned back to her, he almost dropped it in shock. She was tying up her skirts to the height of her knees.

She glanced back at him with a sardonic expression. 'Surely you have seen a lady's legs before, Captain?'

'Yes, but…' he said, then snapped his jaws shut in denial. He had been about to say that he had seen plenty of legs before. He had even seen hers and they were a matter of some in- terest to him. 'You are trying to distract me,' he said with a frown.

'Is it working?' she asked, beaming at him.

'Not enough to make a difference in my fighting,' he said and had to force himself not to smile back. He stole another glance at her. He had barely noticed them when they had been wrapped around his waist, but now that he had time to look, he could see they were a fine set of calves, perhaps the finest he had seen, even clad in silk stockings and hidden at the knees by the ruffles of her raised pet-ticoat. But as she stretched and tested another lunge, she spread them, and the thought of what might be revealed by a tumble made him woozy with desire.

'Are you ready?' she said with a grin, of-fering a salute of her weapon.

'Oh, yes,' he said, not thinking of spar-ring at all.

'En garde,' she replied, dropping easily into a fencer's stance and approaching him.

He did not bother with posing, but ap-proached her, his weapon harmlessly out of line. All the same, he parried her first attack without effort and riposted with a gentle poke to the chest.

She gave a nod of acknowledgement, then backed off, preparing to approach again.

Perhaps he should play the fool and allow her a touch, since it would get him nowhere with a lady if he beat her too often. But as he was considering, she feinted and thrust, scor-ing a touch on his bad shoulder that stung like the devil.

She backed off then, with a shrug of apol-ogy. 'I did not mean to hurt you,' she said with a sheepish grin.

'Then you do not understand the point of swordplay at all,' he replied, annoyed, and raised his weapon, preparing for another attack.

This time, she lunged at him and he deflected it easily. But when he thrust in response, she knocked his blade out of line and darted out of reach.

He stepped back, surprised. 'You are better than I expected, Lady Anne.'

'Miss Fitzroy,' she reminded him with a breathless smile. 'Or Annie. And thank you.'

'If I may offer a suggestion?' he said, then dropped his sword and reached out for her. 'Change your guard, thus. With a light weapon such as this, the control is all in the wrist. Like so.' He took his foil in his right hand to demonstrate and winced at the weight of it, then directed her.

She adjusted her grip as he had shown her and scored another point on him before he knew what had hit him.

Then he attacked in earnest, disarming her. Before he could stop himself, he had raised his sword instinctively for the final slash that would end her.

She gave a yip of surprise and tripped back on her own skirts, falling helpless at his feet.

'Dear God, Annie,' he said, throwing his weapon aside and pulling her to her feet with his good arm. 'I am so sorry.'

'It is all right,' she said, pulling off her mask with a shaky laugh. 'In fact, it was quite exciting to fence with a real master.'

'But I did not mean to threaten you,' he said, trying to stop the shaking feeling of the battle rage still barely contained in him.

'It is all right,' she said, looking deeply into his eyes. 'I trust you.'

Staring back at her, he could feel a flood of calm wash his soul clean of the things he had done. As he had when they had spent the night together, he felt human. Without thinking, he ran his hands up her arms, to convince himself that she was really there and not some spirit he had conjured while searching for forgiveness. 'I am not worthy of your trust,' he admitted.

'You are a hero,' she reminded him. 'And you rescued me, even though I did not want you to. No matter what you tell me, I will trust you.'

But the tone she used did not sound like

trust, it sounded like love, and that was far more than he wanted from her and far more than he could give in return. He should tell her so there could be no misunderstanding. Instead, he heard himself say in a choked voice, 'Thank you.'

Then he pulled her close and she tipped her face up towards his, until their lips met. After two weeks without her, the taste of her was shockingly sweet and had a tenderness he had not felt in her before. This was the kiss of a woman who knew him and who had known him. He opened his mouth slowly and accepted her tentative explorations, giving a sigh of encouragement as she reached out her hands to touch his chest.

Then, there was the sound of her brother making a theatrical level of noise as he came down the hall to interrupt them. 'Has Will come down for breakfast yet? I swear, the man never used to be so soft as to sleep in.'

She withdrew quickly and picked up the sword at her feet, holding it out of line and stepping back. 'He is in here,' she called, 'teaching me tricks that you never would.'

'What the devil?' Her brother took the last few steps into the room in a rush, then relaxed as he saw her armed. 'You made him fight you?' He looked from one to the other of them and Will watched as his suspicion changed to relief.

She nodded vigorously and grinned, both of which helped to disguise her flustered state left from the kiss.

Freddie gave him a resigned look. 'Sometimes I wonder if it is even necessary to worry about her. She clearly does not have the sense necessary to lay down arms and let herself be caught.' Then he gave her another more disapproving look. 'Untie your skirts, you hoyden. We have guests.'

Will resisted the urge to tell her brother what a total menace she was, with or without a sword. But Freddie was looking at her now as though she was a troublesome little sister and not the startlingly beautiful woman the rest of the world knew her to be. It was a wonder that he had trusted the two of them alone together for even a few minutes.

Of course, if she was to be believed, this same brother had taught her to throw a punch...

'How did she do?' Freddie asked, totally missing the danger.

'She needs to keep her tip in line,' he said automatically.

'So I have been telling her,' he said.

'Other than that, not bad,' Will admitted.

'He is very good with a sword,' she said hurriedly. 'Even in his left hand.'

'I would hope so,' Freddie said, 'if he made his living at it.'

It was a good thing that her brother had not noticed the look on Annie's face as she complimented him. The kiss was probably to blame for putting that blush of pleasure on her cheek and the sparkle in her eyes said she was eager for another. It made him wonder why the family insisted that she was opposed to a marriage between them. Didn't she know how good they were together?

But for now, Freddie ignored any hint of intimacy between them and held out his hand to take Annie's sword. 'That is enough for now, little Sister. Go keep my wife company and let the men have their fun.'

Annie removed her coat and, with a last longing look at the foils, disappeared into the morning room to do whatever it was that ladies did when left to themselves.

* * *

He had kissed her.

Annie doodled aimlessly on the paper in front of her, unable to decide what to write to Hattie about the latest developments in her life. Will was here. He had given up the army. And, most importantly, he had kissed her. He had still said nothing about his feelings for her, of course. But he did not seem to dislike her as much as he had when they were in London.

Here in the country, he was quiet, watchful and polite. Some of the tension was gone from him now that he was away from the bustle of the Season and she hoped that meant that he was sleeping better. He was at least getting some beneficial exercise. She could hear the clattering of blades and the men's laughter from the far hallway and wondered if it would be too inappropriate to go and watch.

But that would mean abandoning her sister-in-law and it would be most rude of her.

So, she had waited patiently for luncheon and came into the dining room to find Will and Freddie already there, collars loosened and faces flushed from activity. If possible,

Will looked even more handsome out of uniform than he did in his fine red coat.

When her father took his place at the head of the table, he was holding the day's post and the copy of *The Times* that had come with it.

Annie stared at the paper in fascinated horror, for she had quite forgotten that they had left the city before the release of the uncoveted title of Society's Most Scandalous. Apparently, the moment of revelation had finally arrived.

For the first time in memory, her father did not bother to open the paper, but left it to sit beside his luncheon plate unread.

But not knowing did not improve the mood of anyone sitting there. If anything, it made things worse for the suspense stretched long before them and would likely linger all day.

At last, Annie broke the silence. 'Oh, do get it over with. Let us see what they had to say about me that has not already been said.'

Her father huffed. 'At least we have the comfort of knowing that the award is anticlimactic.' He opened the paper with a rattle and turned to the society pages.

There was another moment of silence and then, he huffed again.

'Do not keep us wondering,' her mother said with a groan. 'Just read it.'

The Duke looked over the paper and, surprising them all, grinned. 'I am sorry to disappoint you, Annie, but you have been beaten.'

'I…am not…' She dropped her fork in shock.

'Miss Felicity Claremont has earned the title,' he said, 'and I quote, "For the concerted effort to ruin the reputation of another young lady and her tendency to bribe servants and gossip about the resulting information gained".'

'Ha.' The single note was all she was able to utter, for the shock was too great and robbed her of speech.

'I wonder who it was that submitted her name?' her mother said, reaching for the paper and scanning it as if there could be more details to uncover.

'Whoever it was, she most heartily deserved it,' Dorothea said with a firm nod of her head. 'My little sister was always a bit of a sneak and this Season, her behaviour has been beyond the pale.'

'But with this revelation, she is likely to

lose her match with the Duke,' Annie said with a frown.

'It is most generous of you to care, after what she did to you,' Freddie replied.

'To have her miserable will not make me any happier,' Annie said.

'But it will likely do her good,' Dorothea replied. 'She is young yet and another year without making a match will give her time to grow out of her foolishness.'

Annie was glad when the topic died out for there was no satisfaction in revenge, although she could not help but feel better that her own name was omitted from this particular honour. But she also noticed that one member of the table was without comment on the subject. When the rest of the family departed from the table, Will lingered and she caught him by the arm.

'It was you who submitted your cousin's name to the paper, wasn't it?'

'What makes you think so?' he said with a noncommittal shrug.

'The details presented were most likely known by a member of the Claremont family,' she said. 'And you had nothing to say on the subject, just now.'

'Perhaps it is because I do not like to waste time with silly, society gossip,' he said.

'Or perhaps it is because you realised who was at fault,' she replied.

'You did not tell me, that night at the club, that you were there to rescue Felicity,' he said.

'You suspected the worst of me,' she reminded him. 'I saw no reason to correct you since you did not want to believe me. And since you had promised not to tell anyone, there was no point in slandering your cousin to you to save my own reputation.'

'Well, I am heartily sorry for not trusting you,' he replied. 'My cousin deserved some punishment for her foolishness, especially since she used that outing as an excuse to turn on you.'

'But you did not have to be the one to administer it,' she said.

'It was not up to me,' he said with a smile. 'The editors of *The Times* were the ones who made the choice. I just provided much-needed information so that they could do so.'

'But to ruin her life…'

'I have ruined her Season. Nothing more than that,' he said with a shrug. 'She is only eighteen and will have a year to learn the importance of good behaviour. By next year, she will be more deserving of the match she makes. Most importantly, she will leave you alone. You do not need any more scandal on top of the story about your parentage.'

'I wish you had thought of that before assaulting Montgomery James,' she said, trying not to glare. 'That will be the talk of London for weeks to come.'

'Someone should have done it a long time ago,' he said, sounding as starchy as ever. 'He deserved punishment for the trick he played on Felicity as well.'

'Of course,' she said with a shake of her head. Perhaps his intervention had not been for her after all. But everyone had heard him mention her name when he had accosted James. Though he might not have meant to involve her, society had made up its mind on the subject.

'And I wish to do more,' he said and she watched as his back straightened and his shoulders squared, as if bracing to receive a blow. If she did not stop him, he was going to offer again. It would be painfully polite and devoid of emotion, just another item on the list of things to do that would settle any wrongs he felt he had committed against her.

He was gathering breath to speak. But before the words could come out, she said, 'That will not be necessary. I assure you, you have done enough. Leave it at that.'

'You are not even going to give me a chance to ask?' he said, holding his hands out to her in a gesture that was both welcome and supplicating.

'Because I know what my answer will be and I want to spare us both,' she said. Then she turned and hurried away.

Chapter Eighteen

'Wait!'

But she did not even slow at the sound of the command. If anything, she walked faster.

'Annie!'

She was practically running now, already on the steps to the bedrooms where he did not dare try to follow her.

'Damn it!'

And now he was swearing, in a house where he was already barely tolerated, frightening the servants and proving to her family that his manners were only fit for the battlefield. But how was he expected to propose to her if she wouldn't be still and let it happen?

He took a breath and wiped his face with his hand as if he could wash away the humiliation just as easily as changing his expression. The whole thing was even harder since they were not supposed to be alone. Was he expected to shout the words up the stairs after her? Was she going to give him any more explanation beyond an unembellished 'no'?

Technically, that was supposed to be enough. But those rules had been designed for men approaching women they had nothing more than a ballroom acquaintance with. If they were practically strangers, the lady was not obligated to enumerate the gentleman's faults to convince him to go away.

But once the relationship had reached a stage of undress, with sweating and groaning and enthusiastic urging on both sides, the answer to a proposal was assumed to be yes. What the hell was she thinking of to refuse him? There was something missing, he was sure. Something he had done, or forgotten to do, and, pernicious beast that she was, she was going to leave him guessing.

If he could catch her, perhaps it would help to remind her that she had enjoyed his company just this morning. It was not as if they mightn't suit, if they tried. He was not very good at any of the things she had liked in London. But she had shown surprising aptitude with a sword. And the sight of her in the flowerbed, trying to shift a sheep...

He smiled. He could not help himself. Thank God he had not laughed at her, or she might never have forgiven him.

And there was the matter of the bedroom, or more accurately, his library couch. They seemed to be very well suited for activities of that nature. Couples all over England married every day knowing far less about each other than they did. Of course, he couldn't say such things aloud in the presence of her family unless he wanted to see her forced down the aisle, willing or not.

Everything about the situation was confusing and he did not like being confused.

But for now, there was nothing to do but while away the afternoon, playing patience and waiting for his next opportunity to see her.

That evening, the Duchess had planned a dinner party, with a few members of the local gentry to round out the table. Though the party was a small one, the prospect left Will feeling uneasy. The seating would be scrambled to give everyone an equal chance at conversation, which meant he might not be seated next to Annie.

It would also put him in the same situation he had been in when they were in London, talking to strangers. And tonight, Dorothea and Freddie would be watching to see if he disgraced himself again as he had at their party. If he wished to make a good impression on the family, he must find a way to conquer his demons and converse politely, no matter the topic.

When he came down to dinner, the family had placed him between a maiden aunt who was hard of hearing and a baron's wife, with Annie across the table to watch over him. She was seated next to the baron and a gentleman named Carruthers, who was a retired colonel but well beyond the age where he might be looking for a wife.

Once again, it appeared that the family was on his side. They had surrounded Annie with ineligible men to improve his chances and given him unobjectionable table companions who were not likely to test his nerves.

But before he could begin a conversation with the older lady on his right, Carruthers ignored Annie and leaned across the table, so eager to get Will's attention that he all but dragged his sleeves through the gravy. 'I hear you are freshly back from Spain.'

'Two months ago,' Will said, then turned his attention to his plate.

'When I was as young as you, I fought in the colonies.'

Some response appeared to be necessary for the man was staring at him expectantly. Before he could answer, Annie spoke, trying to regain her place in the conversation. 'How nice.'

'It was a fine time to be a soldier,' the man said, wolfing down a lamb chop and grinning back at them. 'Of course, the average American had no intelligence to speak of. They were little better than savages. Washington was a crafty devil, though. No match for Napoleon, I am sure.'

'I cannot say,' Will replied, willing himself to be calm and reminding himself that this was a test of his nerve. It had nothing to do with his past, or his feelings about the war.

'You have stories, I'll wager,' the man said with a laugh and then waited for Will to join him in his mirth and contribute his tales of daring.

'Not really,' he said, reaching for his wine glass with his left hand to hide the shaking of his right.

'Oh, come now,' the man said with another laugh. 'You cannot tell me that you have served long and well and have not a single tale to tell from it.'

'None that I would wish to tell when there are ladies present,' he said firmly, then helped himself to some boiled potatoes. In the back of his mind, he could hear artillery fire and the sound of thundering hooves as warhorses bore down on his position.

He forced the thoughts away, focusing on the memory of Annie's hands resting on his heart, brushing his temples, holding his hands. Each gesture she made when they were alone together seemed designed to calm him and he clung to the thought now, like a lifeline thrown to a drowning man. If he could marry her, there would be nothing but night after night of increasing peace.

But to have that future, he must be strong now.

Across the table, Carruthers cleared his

throat to get Will's attention again. 'Later, perhaps, when the ladies have retired.'

'Not even then,' Will said firmly, surprised at the relief he felt, putting the war out of his mind if only for this conversation. 'I have resigned my commission and mean to put that part of my life behind me.' Then he met Carruthers' eyes with an unwavering stare, daring him to continue with his unwelcome questions.

The man huffed once, then turned to the lady at his side and said, 'When I was in the colonies…'

The story was likely to be a long one and Will chose to ignore it, turning to the near-deaf woman at his side and enquiring after her health in a loud, clear tone. The answer drowned out the battle on the other side of the table and allowed him to eat his lamb in peace.

Will Grosvenor had finished his meal without incident.

As the ladies withdrew from the table, leaving the gentlemen to their port, Annie smiled, trying to pretend that this mundane fact was not the success that she knew it to be.

Of course, he was likely to experience more questioning from that boring Colonel Carruthers, but he had handled himself well so far and she had hopes that his success would continue.

Of course, if he was learning to manage his dark moods, he might not need her as he had when they were in London. The thought made her faintly sad. She had enjoyed being there for him and the feeling of closeness that had grown between them during those moments spent alone.

Several more hours passed before the party was over and the guests returned to their homes. By the time she had seen the last one to the door, Will was nowhere to be found. He was probably in his room, alone. There was no way that she could go to him there to see if he needed her. It was simply too scandalous.

But then she remembered that there was an easy way to find him, if he was still struggling with sleeplessness. She waited until Claudine had prepared her for bed, then she slipped a silk wrapper over her nightclothes and tiptoed down to the library to wait for him to arrive.

* * *

A half an hour had passed before the door opened and Will appeared in the doorway, pausing, ready to retreat when he realised that the room was lit and occupied.

'Come in,' she said in a soft voice. 'I have been expecting you.'

'I should not,' he said, preparing to back away.

'But you cannot sleep,' she finished for him. 'Come in. Stay with me a while.'

'Perhaps we can relive my glorious war stories,' he said with a bitter laugh, looking more tired than he had at dinner.

'He did not know what he was asking,' Annie said softly.

'And do you?' he said, turning to give her a sceptical look.

'I understand that war is uglier than I can imagine and I am glad that you are not going back to it,' she said. 'I do not like to think of you there.'

'While I am glad of your approval, I am still haunted by the fact that others are fighting in my stead,' he said with a shake of his head. 'And fellows like Carruthers will always be there to remind me of my failure.'

'You are not a failure,' she insisted, patting the cushion at her side.

He shook his head. 'I do not know what I am any more. But at least I was able to last through dinner without running for the garden. Perhaps hanging up my sword will do me good.'

'And why did you resign your commission?' she asked, watching as the muscles of his bad arm tensed in response.

'We both know why,' he replied. 'I have responsibilities here.'

'Responsibilities,' she said, letting the single word hang between them. 'If you mean me, I would prefer you not think that way. I have no intention of marrying you or anyone else.'

'Do not talk rot,' he said, surprising her with a display of temper. 'It is one thing to refuse me and quite another to decide that no man in England is worthy of your hand.'

'It is not a matter of worthiness,' she said, wondering how he could be so blind. 'When I left London, no one was willing to stand with me.'

'Except me,' he reminded her.

The truth of it did much to undercut her argument, but she went on, all the same. 'Except for you. You were a true friend to me.'

'A friend,' he said in a dull tone and sat down beside her.

'Yes,' she said, struggling to find a name for what they had that, from his side at least, did not seem to be love.

Then he leaned closer and, as she had since the first night they'd met, she felt the magnetic pull to be near him. Now that she was sure he was all right, she should leave him alone and go back upstairs. Instead, she was frozen in place, waiting for him to make the next move.

She had been sitting with her feet tucked up on the couch, and he thrust his hand under the hem of her nightdress to cover them. 'You are cold,' he said, stroking them gently.

She took a slow breath, trying not to shudder in excitement as the warmth of his touch spread through her body.

'Very cold if you call what we feel for each other mere friendship,' he said, withdrawing his hand for a moment and watching her look of disappointment. Then he touched her again.

'I have not got a night's sleep since the night we were together,' he said.

A stronger woman would remind him that he was also not sleeping before they had been together. Why would a single night with her bring about a change? But that imaginary paragon would not have come down here to wait for him, so they could be alone together. She reached out to him, touching his temples. 'I know something that will help.'

He pulled away from her, shocked. 'Did you learn nothing the last time we were together?'

She smiled. 'I learned quite a bit, actually.'

'Yet when I try to offer for you, you refuse me.' Then he ignored the danger and closed his eyes, leaning into her touch.

'What we share when we are alone is not enough to make a lifetime on,' she said, stroking his hair and guiding his head to rest on her breast. She massaged his brow, drawing circles with her thumbs, feeling the furrows in his forehead relax at her touch.

He lay against her innocently for a moment, then reached a hand to the buttons of her nightdress, opening them and spreading the fabric until his face rested against bare skin. His lips began to move on her then, his mouth hungry for her, his hands greedy as they moved up her leg.

'You are a witch,' he whispered. 'I cannot think straight when I am with you. We should not be doing this.' But then his teeth caught her nipple and she no longer cared what was right or wrong. She wanted him. She stopped her caresses to fumble with the buttons on his shirt and his hands swept up her body from underneath, stripping her gown and the wrapper away to leave her naked and kneeling on the couch before him.

Then he stripped his shirt away as well and she saw for the first time the torn flesh of his shoulder and the recently healed bullet wound. She kissed it gently, then ran her fingers over the raised scars, willing his pain away.

He sighed at her touch, then held her to him, skin to skin as he kissed her mouth, desire mingled with gratitude. She allowed her hands to rove over his arms and back, revelling in the feel of his hard chest pressed against her, rejoicing in the strength of him, the solidness and the overwhelming knowledge that, as long as she was in his arms, nothing or no one could hurt her.

Then he pushed her away and slid down her body to kneel on the floor before her, settling his face between her legs, kissing her in a way that was both unexpected and delicious.

'Does this feel like friendship to you?' he murmured the words into her thigh before taking the most sensitive part of her into his mouth and sucking. She could feel him undoing the buttons of his breeches with short sharp tugs that matched the pull on her body and she moaned with shock and desire at the clever movement of his tongue against her sex and the knowledge of what was to come.

As his mouth moved on her, the need to wait for him warred with the desire to give in and suddenly, she was lost in a flood of sensation, gripping his shoulders and riding out wave after wave of pleasure until she dropped back against the cushions, helpless and sated.

He raised his head and smiled in satisfaction, then rose and kicked free of his breeches, standing before her naked and magnificent. 'After this, you will be mine,' he said, 'in all ways that matter.'

'All ways but one,' she answered back on a gasp.

He pushed her back on to the couch and covered her with his body, letting his sex find its home inside hers. And for a time, they forgot the future and lost themselves in the joy of the moment. He moved in long controlled strokes and she felt her own body tighten on him as she rocked her hips into his, her breasts pressed so tightly into his scarred body that she could hardly breathe.

But it didn't matter. She didn't need anything but him. So she willed him to feel her love as she gave herself to him, her body shuddering as she lost control again. He followed her a moment later, sagging against her as he released.

Slowly, they sank back on to the sofa together still wrapped in each other's arms, listening to their own heartbeats in the silence that followed their lovemaking. It was a moment of such perfection that she wished it would never end.

Then he kissed her again and whispered, 'Do we have an understanding?'

'I beg your pardon?' she said, as the afterglow disappeared and reality came crashing back.

'We will be announcing our engagement to your family tomorrow,' he said with his usual, superior overconfidence.

'We will not,' she said, pulling away from him and reaching for her nightgown.

'You cannot deny that there is attraction between us,' he said in a voice that was far too reasonable, given what they had just been doing.

'But I have no idea whether it is more or less than I might experience with another man,' she said and was pleased to see his face clouding with jealousy.

'It would not be the same,' he insisted. 'And I am not going to allow you to roam about the countryside, experimenting on the matter. We have lain together twice. We are playing a dangerous game and this cannot keep happening without some promise of marriage.'

'Then you should have discussed it with me before,' she said, 'because I have no intention of marrying you just because of this.'

Now, he not just angry, but baffled. 'What is your problem with me? It is clear that you are not repelled. You are more kind and gentle than any woman I have ever been with.'

'And how many women is that?' she said, strangely curious.

'That is not the point,' he said quickly. 'What I mean to say is that we are very well suited when we are alone together.'

'But that is not the only thing that is important,' she insisted.

'What else could possibly matter?' he said. 'I have enough money to provide for you. I have the approval of your family. I want to take care of you and can tell that you care for me.'

'And yet I do not want to marry you,' she said, frustrated that he did not understand. It would be so easy to tell him the words he had to say to win her. But then he would parrot them back to her without meaning them and she would never be able to believe him again.

'You are being unreasonable,' he said, looking at her with a patronising smile.

'Then I do not see why you would want me,' she replied.

'After what we have done, honour requires…'

'Please, do not prattle on about honour,' she said, pulling on her nightgown and tying her robe tight about her. 'I have refused you. If you truly have honour, there is nothing more to say on the matter.' Then, before he could speak again, she ran from the library and back to her room.

Chapter Nineteen

She had refused him again.

After she left him, he had sat steaming at the thought of her. She was unreasonable, infuriating, and yet utterly delicious. He had half a mind to trail her down the hall and beg her to come back so they could carry on as they'd been doing, making love until the dawn broke and she was too tired to deny him her hand. Surely she must see that, at night at least, they belonged together.

As for the rest of the time? He was not so sure. But there was no law that said a husband and wife had to spend every hour of the day in each other's pocket. The night would be enough.

He pulled on his shirt and did up his breeches and walked back to his room with a book to explain his wandering. Then he climbed into his bed and fell into a surprisingly deep sleep. Maddening though she was, she eased his mind unlike any other diversion he had found.

He had dreamed of her and woke hugging his pillow, his face pressed into the linen in an open-mouthed kiss.

It was embarrassing. But at least he was not too exhausted to spend the day, as Freddie had suggested, in fishing for pike on the lake. And he would need to have his wits about him, since the solitude would give the fellow the chance to question him on his progress with his sister.

He needed time to prove to everyone, Annie included, that he was the man they all needed him to be. A day on the lake would give him a chance to find his balance and cool his temper. Most of all, he needed time away from Annie, so that evidence of what they had done did not shine from his face like a beacon each time he looked at her.

But when he and Freddie reached the front hall on their way to the door, they were confronted by the last woman he wanted to see.

No matter how late their night had been, this morning she was fresh and pretty in a yellow muslin dress. She was also capable of looking through him as if he did not matter to her at all.

Instead, her full attention was on her brother and she glared at him as if he had committed some treasonous offence. 'Where do you think you are going?' It was an odd way to begin since the bamboo rods waiting by the door for them should have made it obvious that they were headed to the lake.

'We are going to bring back dinner,' Freddie said, giving his sister a dashing smile.

'Not Old Ned,' she said, looking at back at him in annoyance.

'If he allows himself to be caught,' Freddie said. 'I quite fancy pike and there is not a finer one in the lake than him.'

'Then I am going, too,' she announced.

'Fishing,' Will said, unable to keep the doubt from showing in his voice.

'You are not,' Freddie replied to his sister, then turned to Will. 'She thinks, since she has been out in a boat with me before, that she is something of an angler.' He turned back to Annie again and added, 'But now that she is grown, she should know that it is not appropriate.'

'A Season in London has not left me unable to handle a fishing pole,' she said and braced her hands on her hips, stepping ahead of them to block the way to the door.

Freddie gave Will a worried glance, then looked back at Annie and said in a clipped tone, 'It is not ladylike,'

'I will show you what a lady looks like,' she said through gritted teeth. Then she turned on Will. 'He promised last year that I would be coming along on any fishing trips. I have been chasing Old Ned since I was old enough to pick up a rod. I have no intention of letting the two of you take him without my at least being there.'

'There is no guarantee that we will catch a fish of any sort,' Will said, quite reasonably.

'Or you could catch Old Ned,' she said, 'without giving me my chance at him.'

Freddie sighed, then turned to Will. 'I know this is unusual, but would you mind if my little sister accompanied us on our fishing trip?'

'Not at all,' Will said, reminding himself

that seeing Annie and being amiable was the real object of this visit.

She held up a finger. 'I will change. Wait here just a moment.' Then she was running for the stairs.

Freddie let out a groan of frustration and said, 'I apologise for this. I know that you wish to spend time with my sister, but I am sure this is not what you had in mind.'

'It is quite all right,' he assured his friend. 'I am not unfamiliar with the ways of women and quite prepared to make allowances.' Knowing Annie as he did, he could imagine the costume she probably thought was appropriate for pike fishing. Green muslin, perhaps, with deep ruffles that would be ruined when trailed in the water. For good measure, he imagined a dainty parasol to keep the sun off her nose. It would take the better part of an hour to get her hair right and her bonnet tied, and by then the fish would be gone or asleep or whatever it was that fish did to become unattainable.

To his surprise, she appeared at the top of the stairs in less than ten minute, and took them at a gallop, skidding to a stop in front of him.

The costume she had chosen was nothing like he'd imagined. She was wearing a plain cotton gown and a straw bonnet. Sensible boots completed the outfit. Her hair was tied back from her face and mostly hidden under the hat. He noticed a light dusting of freckles on her nose that had either appeared from the country sun or had been hidden by powder in the city.

Why should he find it so strange to see her dressed for fishing? That was what they were going to do, after all. She was always dressed appropriately for the occasion.

He had just never imagined her like this. And seeing her thus, he realised that he'd always assumed her utter perfection was some sort of façade to hide flaws in person or character. Even after seeing underneath her gown, he had imagined her as some sort of temptress and not the red-blooded, pleasantly pretty girl that she was.

'It seems we have caught a fish already,' she said, staring at him with frustration. 'Close your mouth, Captain, before someone sticks a hook in it.' Then she flounced past him and grabbed one of the poles and led the way towards the lake.

When they arrived at the edge of the water, there was a small boat waiting for them, already stocked with a bucket of bait and a linen-covered hamper for luncheon. Annie hitched up her skirts and clambered out on to the little dock it was tied to, then down into the boat, taking a seat in the prow.

He should have offered her an arm. But she had no need and he needed both of his to get down into the boat himself. He sat in the stern, staring in annoyance at the oars as Freddie took them and propelled them out on to the water. If Will wanted to show the lady his worth, he should have been the one to row. But the effort would have been quite beyond him.

Perhaps it was his weakness that made her refuse him. She was looking past her brother at him and there was no sign in her expression that there was anything between the two of them beyond a friendly acquaintance. 'There,' she said, spreading her hands to encompass the scene. 'Isn't this delightful?'

'Says the creature who is expending no effort,' grunted Freddie, giving another pull or two and letting them drift the rest of the way towards the centre of the pond. He glanced around him as if gauging the spot. 'This is about right, isn't it?'

She gave the shore a calculating glance. 'There is the fallen tree and we are a few boat lengths past the drop off. He is waiting right below us.'

'May I help you bait your hook, Miss Fitz-roy?' Will said, remembering that there was still a chance for gallantry.

'A person who can't touch a worm doesn't belong in the boat,' Freddie said, missing the point of the offer.

'Too true,' the lady replied, reaching into the bucket and pulling out a large worm and hooking it like an experienced fisher. Then she gave her brother a critical look. 'The guts of last night's trout would do just as well.'

'The cook threw them away,' he replied and they both let out a remorseful sigh.

Freddie baited his own hook and passed the bucket on to Will. Once the lines were in the water, they settled down to silent con-templation.

When she had invited herself along on this expedition, he had imagined the outing would be ruined with girlish chatter. Not that listening to Annie would be annoying, he reminded himself. If he was preparing to subject himself to a lifetime of it, he should not think of his wife's speech as an irritant.

He had been wrong, as he had been about so many things. She was as quiet as a man and quieter than some of those. Her silence gave him a chance to admire her as he tipped his hat over his eyes, pretending to nap.

Though he had done so when they had lain together, he had found it hard to imagine relaxing in her presence while awake. In London, she had been a symbol of everything in society that made him ill at ease. But here, she was a different person.

Then there was a tug on her line and her stillness evaporated into a flurry of movement. 'I have him.' She pulled back and the pole bent. 'I have something at least.'

Her brother glanced up sceptically. 'Most likely you are caught on a log.'

'The log is fighting back,' she said, giving a yank to set the hook. 'Ready the net.'

'You are not strong enough to bring him in by yourself, if that is him,' her brother said, shifting in her direction and making the boat pitch.

'That does not mean I can't try,' she said, bracing herself against the side and giving another tug on the line.

'Here. Give me that rod,' Freddie said, making a lunge for it.

'Not on your life,' she replied, giving a mighty pull. A few yards out from the boat, a large fish crested the water and disappeared again.

'Be careful,' Will said, grabbing the stern as the boat rocked again.

The squabbling siblings paid him no mind as they tussled for control of the fishing pole. When Annie did not release the rod to him, Freddie gave her an ungentlemanly shove and took it, pulling the fish towards the boat. But the force of his grab was all it took to knock her fully off balance and she toppled backwards out of the boat and into the lake.

'Annie!' As she disappeared below the surface, Will's own breath stopped as if willing her to hold hers until he could get to her. If he did not and she drowned…

She could not die. She simply could not. Without his love, there was no point in living!

Love. He had not told her he loved her. He had not known it until this moment. But now that he did, it was as if he had loved her from the first moment they'd met. That maddening, intriguing, infuriating woman who he did not understand and could not live without.

He had to save her. He was on his feet, struggling out of his coat, ready to dive in after her when her head popped up a few feet away.

'Annie,' he said again, too frightened for her to say more.

She waved a wet arm in his direction and shouted, 'Never mind me. Get the gaff. See to the fish.'

'Come here,' he said, exasperated, and reached out with his good arm, ready to haul her back over the side.

'I am fine,' she repeated, swimming to the side of the boat and holding on. 'See to Freddie and that damned fish.'

For a moment, he was too shocked to move. It was not that he had never seen a woman swear before. The camp followers in Spain said all kinds of things that would shock a normal man. But he had never seen a true lady, such as Annie, use language like that.

Of course, he had never seen a lady hanging from the side of a boat.

He wanted to kiss her. Right then and there. He had wanted to kiss her before. Damn it to hell, he liked kissing her. But even in their most passionate moments, he had never felt this over-the-moon urge to gather her in his arms and kiss her until he had shocked the world.

It was a surprise. But then, everything about her was a surprise. He could spend a lifetime trying to understand her and she would never cease to amaze him. Then he did as she said and readied the net for what appeared to be a very nice-sized pike.

'Is it Old Ned?' she demanded from the water, totally oblivious to what was happening.

'I do not think so,' Freddie said with a frown, equally impervious. 'It is a very fine fish though.'

'Damn,' she muttered again. 'If I had to get soaked, you could have at least had the decency to push me aside over the right fish. I am sure I could have landed this fish by myself.' She looked up at Will then with an entirely different, sweeter expression than she might have used on any suitor to make him forget her earlier behaviour. 'You may help me in now, Captain Grosvenor, if it is not too much trouble.'

'Call me Will,' he blurted, feeling his face set in an idiotic grin.

'Will,' she said, giving him a dubious look in return. She held out her hand to remind him of her current predicament.

He did as she asked and used his good arm to pull her back over the side, and she landed, rather like the fish had, soaking wet and flopping on the floor of the boat. She had lost her boots in the water, probably kicking them off in the struggle to stay afloat, and two very attractive feet poked out from under the wet skirts that clung to her legs.

She was adorable.

In true, brotherly fashion, Freddie looked down at her and laughed, showing no sympathy at all. 'You asked to come along.'

'And I am not complaining,' she reminded him, letting him help her back up the boat to her seat in front where she looked down to admire the fish. 'And you must admit, I hooked us a fine dinner.'

'You did not pull him in, though,' Freddie replied.

A mild argument ensued about which of the two could claim the catch and, during it, Will looked steadfastly out at the water, still grinning. Perhaps her brother was used to seeing his sister with her gown clinging to her wet body, but Will suspected that Freddie would not be amused to see him taking an interest in some of the finer points that were now on display.

Though he wanted to. By God, he wanted to drink her in as if he had never seen her before and was never going to see her again. But he did not have to look at her now. Even with his eyes closed, he could imagine a lifetime with her, dressed in silks, rags, or nothing at all. He would be equally happy, any way he could have her.

He needed to tell her how he felt.

But not in the presence of her brother and a dead fish. He could not exactly drop his feelings into the middle of the conversation that was currently going on without him and which seemed to involve the finer points of pike over trout over freshwater salmon.

Freddie was rowing towards shore and Will wanted to grab the oars from his hands and pull faster and damn the pain in his shoulder. He needed to get back to the house and into a clean suit so he could propose.

Once out of the boat, they made their way back to the house, Annie racing ahead of them, eager to get out of her wet clothes. As she disappeared upstairs Freddie said, 'You do not have sisters, do you?'

'No,' Will admitted, staring after her, hungry for just one more sight of her.

'Then you do not know what trouble they can be,' he said with a smile. 'It was worse when there were two of them. Hattie was not so much bother, because of the injury to her leg. But they managed to gang up on me, all the same.'

'I see,' said Will, though he did not see at all. How could it be any trouble at all to spend time with Annie?

'Come into the library. We will not see her again for the rest of the day. Even if we do, she smells of pond water and we do not want her tracking through the house after us.'

'Until later, then,' Will said, smiling to himself, finally looking away from the stairs.

* * *

It was not until she got upstairs that Annie noticed her appearance and when she did, she was mortified. Her bonnet had wilted, her hair was full of weeds, her stockings, torn and dirty, were pooled at her ankles, and her dress was stuck to her body in a way that was positively indecent.

It was no wonder that Will had not looked at her even once after he'd got her back into the boat. Of the two of them, the fish was far more attractive and he'd kept his eyes on it the whole trip back to land.

Or perhaps he was still angry with her after last night. It didn't matter, she reminded herself. It was not as if she wanted to marry him. She was not going to yoke herself to a man who saw her as another duty, just like the one he had previously owed to the King. Despite what he and her family might think, duty was not enough to make a life on.

Duty and passion, of course. She shivered. When they were together at night, there was certainly no denying the chemistry between them. But he had admitted that there had been other women in his life and he had no doubt felt something similar when he had been with them. Though it was wonderful for her, she had no idea if this was a feeling that would last beyond the honeymoon for either of them.

While Claudine drew her a bath, she imagined what it might be like to spend evenings with him, staring resolutely at the floor, thinking about what he was missing by spending time with her. It would be unbearable. She needed armour before she saw him again, something to prove to him that she was not the dripping mess that had followed him back to the house.

'What do you wish to wear this evening?' Claudine said, shuffling through the gowns in the wardrobe as Annie sunk deep into the copper bathtub.

'My best dinner gown,' she said, splashing water on her muddy toes. 'Something that will make me forget this afternoon happened.'

Except for the fish, of course.

Chapter Twenty

By evening, his Annie had disappeared.

Of course, she was not strictly his, as yet. But Will had begun to think of her as such the moment he'd heard her swear. He had suspected that the woman he'd met in London had such hidden depths. He should have known better. No woman who kissed as she did was as shallow as Lady Anne first appeared.

He should have known when he had seen her wrestling with the sheep, or when she had challenged him with a sword. But he had thought that those things were aberrations. He had not expected to find an entirely different women hidden inside the diamond of the London Season.

He thought of her, rising out of the lake like

Venus rising from the waves, if Venus had been exceptionally angry and rather muddy, and he smiled. And he had known that that particular vision could not last. She would catch her death if she did not change.

But he had not expected her to bounce back to what she had been in London, like a metal spring that retained its form no matter how you pulled on it. Tonight, she was as beautiful as she had ever been, her hair piled on top of her head in an elaborate concoction of braids and ribbons and wearing a gown of blue with a bodice trimmed in silk flowers.

She was lovely both ways and if he could get her to marry him, he was a lucky man. He sighed happily.

She looked at him in alarm. 'Is something the matter?'

'Not any more,' he assured her.

Now she was looking at him in confusion, her brow furrowed and her mouth set in a frown.

As he looked back at her, he felt a curious bubbling in his spirit, unlike anything he had felt in ages. The hole is his soul was filling with something that felt like champagne. He had been older than time when he met her, dying from the inside. But somehow, it had all changed.

'You look ill,' she added.

'Well, I am not.'

And then the footman set a dressed pike on the centre of the table and all he could think of was the look on her face as she had demanded he help with the damned fish. He was smiling. No. He was about to laugh. For the thought of the goddess he had loved last night, in the water and cursing, was both touching and funny.

'Is there a problem, Captain?' she whispered, now more alarmed than confused.

'Please,' he said, loud enough for the rest of the table to hear, 'call me William. And I am fine, thank you. Very well. The pike is excellent, by the way.'

She shook her head and went back to her meal, taking a large helping of the fish.

'Annie fell in the water while we were fishing for it,' Freddie announced to the room.

'Freddie pushed me,' Annie added.

The Duchess shook her head in a way that said she had heard all this before. 'I had hoped that, with marriage, you would have outgrown such behaviour, Frederick.'

In response, he shrugged and helped himself to the pike. 'Will did not mind, I am sure.'

'Not at all,' Will said and gave Annie a wink.

'Is there something in your eye?' she said, baffled.

Surely he had not been as joyless as that. No wonder she had refused him. 'No,' he replied. 'And call me Will.'

'William,' she corrected, glancing nervously around the table.

He gave her an encouraging smile and took a bite of fish.

'Have you given any more thought to your future, Grosvenor?' This comment came from Annie's true father at the end of the table. The fellow had obviously sensed a change in him and was giving him a chance to either impress the lady or hang himself with his own tongue.

'Actually, yes,' he said, searching his mind for a way to organise the half-formed ideas he'd had in London. 'There is a need for patronage at the St Michael's Soldiers' Hospital. The place is grim and does nothing to help soldiers once their physical wounds are healed. I thought, perhaps, some sort of school or employment bureau...'

'That is a brilliant idea,' Annie said, giving him a smile that warmed him to his toes. 'And Uncle Benedict has promised me that next Season, I shall receive money held in trust...'

'Intended as a dowry,' the man said quickly and gave Will a sharp look.

'But if I do not want to marry, you would want the money to go to a good purpose,' she said. 'And I can think of none better—'

'Perhaps Miss Fitzroy and I can speak, after dinner,' Will interrupted, making his intentions clear to everyone in the room.

'I... I...' Now she looked trapped. It was the last look he wanted to see on the face of a woman he thought of as his soul's mate.

Will held his breath, waiting to see if she would refuse him again at the table or allow him to say his piece in private.

Then she took a deep breath and nodded. 'We will speak after dinner.'

He could tell by the smiles on the faces around the table that this time there would be no chaperon for their conversation. His battle was half won and her family was standing with him.

But he had not felt so nervous staring down Napoleon's cannons as he did facing Annie now. Perhaps it was because a 'no' from her tonight would be as final as death. If she could not bring herself to love him, then there was nothing more for it, he would have to leave and bother her no more.

And, looking at her now, the situation did not seem promising. She looked so worried by the impending discussion and set her fork to the side as if she could no longer stomach eating. It did not bode well for him. But hopefully, this time he could find the words that would change her mind.

She had surrendered.

At least, that was how it must have appeared to both Will and the family. Agreeing to meet with him in private was tantamount to accepting a proposal. It shouldn't have been, of course. But she could not exactly tell the family that they had been meeting in private for weeks and doing things far more serious than talking. Even so, they had not managed to come to an agreement.

Of course, now he had suggested helping with the hospital. And that was certainly work that she wanted to continue for herself and encourage in him. What he had described was a far better idea than his plan to go back and continue fighting. She could not help but get excited at his idea for an employment agency.

But she had not thought, as she spoke, that her enthusiasm would put her in a position where she had to marry to carry her plans out. Perhaps, if she did marry him, it would be best for everyone. He would have the money for his plans. She would have a respectable marriage that protected her reputation. Her parents would be happy.

And maybe if they worked together at the hospital, he would grow to have some feeling for her other than desire.

When dinner ended, the ladies retired to the sitting room and the Duchess fussed over her appearance, pinching her cheeks to put roses into them. Then, surprisingly, she gave Annie's bodice a tug downwards.

Annie pulled it back up. 'Mother,' she said in a warning tone.

The woman gave her a wry smile. 'If you know as much about fishing as you pretend to, then you know you must bait the hook before you catch anything.'

'I do not think it is necessary in this case,' she said, embarrassed.

'Suit yourself,' her mother said with a shrug, then gave her a kiss on the cheek. 'Now, I think it is time for Dorothea and myself to find something else to occupy our time. Cards in the library, perhaps.'

Dorothea came to her then and kissed her as well. 'We will be nearby if you need us.'

'Thank you,' she said, wishing she could tell them that all this fussing was not necessary. The proposal would be as matter of fact as everything else the Captain had done and she would probably accept it because she was tired of fighting the tide of opinion on her choice of husband.

Then the door opened and Will stepped into the room, closing it behind the two giggling women who were hurrying away from them.

Annie stared at the door for a moment, struggling with the urge to call them back, just as Dorothea had suggested she do. They were both so happy for her. She did not have the heart to tell them that she could not do this. It would make her miserable, but this time, she would force herself to say yes.

She turned to Will and gave him a watery smile, fumbling in her pocket for a handkerchief.

Before she could find one, he was across the room to her and had produced his own and put it in her hand. 'Tears,' he said, shaking his head. 'This does not bode well for me.'

'I don't know what has come over me,' she said, dabbing at her eyes.

'You have been under a lot of pressure,' he said, as if unaware that he was adding to it.

'That is no excuse,' she said, straightening her spine and preparing for what was to come. 'Let's get this over with.'

He gave a nervous laugh. 'I suppose I deserve this response, considering the quality of my previous attempts to propose.'

'They were very pragmatic,' she admitted.

'I am a sensible man,' he said. 'I was, at least.'

'Was?' His plan for St Michael's had sounded very sensible indeed.

'Circumstances have changed,' he said, wetting his lips and looking as nervous as she felt.

'In what way?' she asked.

'I realised something, as we were fishing

today. Something unexpected,' he said, pausing again. 'You are different than I thought you were.'

'If this is about my falling into the lake,' she said, suddenly annoyed, 'that could have happened to anyone. Especially since I was pushed. I do not think it is fair of you to hold it against me.'

'I do not blame you for that,' he said hurriedly. And then, his face took on the same curious expression he had worn at dinner. 'It is just that, I had never seen you in quite that light before. It was...'

'Embarrassing? I am well aware of that. But we cannot always look our best, can we?'

'I have seen you look dishevelled before,' he reminded her. 'The day Nelson jumped on you, for example. And the incident with the sheep...' He smiled.

'That was not my fault either. Neither of those,' she added, then muttered, 'I cannot believe you are going to mention that da—'

Before she had finished her thought, he lifted her bodily from the floor, brought her mouth to his and kissed her. It was quick and close-mouthed, a playful kiss that was over as quickly as if had begun. Then he set her down again, staring at her with an expression she could not remember seeing before. 'I love your mouth,' he said and grinned.

She gasped in surprise, her earlier rant almost forgotten. Had he really used *that word* so casually that she could hardly credit its value? It was just an expression, she was sure. For why, of all moments, would he have such feelings now?

'You are just trying to keep me from being angry,' she said, eyes narrowed. 'Do not do it again.'

'I am sorry,' he said, with an expression he probably thought was contrition, but which still looked quite intimidating. 'I am not very good at this.'

'At what?'

'At telling you how I feel,' he said on a rush of air that made it seem that this partial admission was a struggle.

'You feel for me?' she said, feeling just as breathless.

'I did not realise it until today. When you fell into the water...' He shrugged. 'You are a miracle and I was a fool not to notice it earlier. I have been prattling on about duty, when I should have opened my heart and let you in,' he said, holding out a hand to her.

'Duty is what you know best,' she allowed, still afraid to smile at him as he was smiling at her.

'I should have known it was you for me, always, from the first moment we met. And when you told me to get the damned fish, I realised that there was no other woman that I could ever love.'

'The fish,' she said, sitting on the sofa as all the strength left her legs. It made no sense at all. But it was what she had been waiting for weeks to hear from him.

He sank to his knees in front of her. 'Please, tell me that you feel the same.'

It felt as if her heart was swelling in her chest until it was impossible to breathe, much less speak. At last, she said, 'I was afraid to say it, feeling like a fool because you did not care for me.'

'I was the fool,' he assured her. 'I thought we were too different, even though you showed me over and over by your actions that you were perfect for me. Of course, you also kept refusing me,' he added with a smile.

'Because I did not want to marry a man who did not return my love,' she said.

'Your love,' he said with a happy sigh. 'I did not know I had it and did not know how to give it back. But that is changed now.' He took her hand then and kissed it once before looking deeply into her eyes. 'Will you have me, Annie? I am yours in any case, but will you be mine as well?'

He was smiling at her again. It was not that he had never smiled before today, but there had always been something behind the expression, as if it was a mask that hid deeper pain. Now, when he looked at her, there was a light of hope in his eyes, as if he could see the future she had dreamed of with him.

'Yes,' she whispered and leaned forward to kiss him on the mouth.

He allowed her only a moment, before pulling away and saying. 'No more of that. Your entire family is waiting outside that door for us to announce the good news.'

'Let them wait,' she said, pulling him forward for a proper kiss. 'Let them wait.'

* * * * *

Read on for a teaser from the
first book in the
Society's Most Scandalous series,
How to Woo a Wallflower
by Virginia Heath.

Hattie's temper was calming. That was obvious by the way she gently put the paperweight back in its proper place rather than slamming it down with the same force with which she had picked it up.

Part of him wanted to believe his mere presence helped soothe her as hers did him. The other part—the more reasoned and measured part—understood he wasn't being fair in that wish. Just because she had been there in his hour of need it did not give him the right to dominate her hours.

She exhaled as she shook her head, exasperation leaking from every pore. 'I am certainly very different from who I was then, too—except in my brother's eyes. To him, I am worse than the child I was. So fragile, pathetic with my dratted limp, and so suggestible and ignorant of the harsh realities of life that I must be cosseted at every juncture. It is as if he doesn't know me at all.'

'I think I said as much verbatim to him.'

'Thank you.'

Her smile warmed his soul and destroyed it at the same time.

'But I doubt he listened. He is too wedded to his outrage. Determined to see seduction at every turn. As if you would seduce me now!' She scoffed at that, her eyes dipping as she shook her head. 'Me, of all people! How stupid is he to consider such nonsense?'

Jasper couldn't decide if she had discounted any chance of that because of his reputation, his new circumstances, her lack of attraction to him or her own self-consciousness about her 'dratted leg'.

'So what else did the cretin say when he read you the Riot Act?'

'That I am not to consort with you alone in public ever again.'

She was silent for a moment and then her temper surged afresh. 'How dare he? How *dare* he? I am a grown woman, nearing the age of majority, and whomever I choose to *"consort"* with is no business of his!'

Jasper reached across the table to cover her hand with his, needing to touch her even though he had no right. As always, the innocent contact still reminded him that he was a man.

'We have become fast friends you and I, yes?' She stared at their hands for a moment before nodding. 'Then as your friend, one who cares deeply about your welfare, I have to concede your brother is right. You are a born rescuer to your core and I adore that about you, but my life is complicated. My reputation has always been precarious to say the least.'

'I do not care about that.'

'Of course you don't. But I do.' He laced his fingers though hers. 'So I shan't be importuning you again in public. I will not add fuel to a fire that could burn you to cinders but only scorch me. You have already been through enough pain, Hattie, and I will not be the cause of more.'

COMING SOON!

We really hope you enjoyed reading this book.
If you're looking for more romance, be sure to
head to the shops when new books are
available on

Thursday 24th
November

To see which titles are coming soon, please visit

millsandboon.co.uk/nextmonth

MILLS & BOON®

Coming next month

CHALLENGING THE BROODING EARL
Lucy Ashford

"You."

Oh, no. Merryn's heart sank to the soles of her buttoned boots because it was the man from the fair. Hearing the door close softly behind her, she realized the butler had retreated after doubtlessly taking in that short, damning greeting.

"My lord," she said at last. She made a formal curtsy; Liam, following her lead, gave a little bow. "This is a surprise to me also."

Her voice was calm and that amazed her, because inside she was so shaken that she felt sick. What kind of cruel joke had fate played on her this time?

"Please enlighten me," he said. His voice—every bit as rich and deep as she remembered—was etched with incredulity. "Is this some kind of blackmail, perhaps? Are you here to ask for money?"

"Of course not!" She clamped down on her anger while thinking, *Hateful, hateful man.* "I'm actually here on legitimate business, my lord."

"Really?" There was sheer disbelief in that one word.

"Yes! My name is Miss Merryn Hythe. This is my brother, Liam—and I'm here to claim Liam's inheritance."

You could have heard a pin drop. It was the earl who

finally broke the silence. "Well," he spoke exceedingly softly, "you've been plotting hard since last night, haven't you?"

Continue reading
CHALLENGING THE BROODING EARL
Lucy Ashford

Available next month
www.millsandboon.co.uk

MILLS & BOON

THE HEART OF ROMANCE

A ROMANCE FOR EVERY READER

MODERN
Prepare to be swept off your feet by sophisticated, sexy and seductive heroes, in some of the world's most glamourous and romantic locations, where power and passion collide.

HISTORICAL
Escape with historical heroes from time gone by. Whether your passion is for wicked Regency Rakes, muscled Vikings or rugged Highlanders, awaken the romance of the past.

MEDICAL
Set your pulse racing with dedicated, delectable doctors in the high-pressure world of medicine, where emotions run high and passion, comfort and love are the best medicine.

True Love
Celebrate true love with tender stories of heartfelt romance, from the rush of falling in love to the joy a new baby can bring, and a focus on the emotional heart of a relationship.

Desire
Indulge in secrets and scandal, intense drama and plenty of sizzling hot action with powerful and passionate heroes who have it all: wealth, status, good looks…everything but the right woman.

HEROES
Experience all the excitement of a gripping thriller, with an intense romance at its heart. Resourceful, true-to-life women and strong, fearless men face danger and desire - a killer combination!

To see which titles are coming soon, please visit

millsandboon.co.uk/nextmonth

JOIN US ON SOCIAL MEDIA!

Stay up to date with our latest releases, author news and gossip, special offers and discounts, and all the behind-the-scenes action from Mills & Boon...

 @millsandboon

 @millsandboonuk

 facebook.com/millsandboon

 @millsandboonuk

It might just be true love...

GET YOUR ROMANCE FIX!

Get the latest romance news,
exclusive author interviews, story
extracts and much more!

blog.millsandboon.co.uk